RETREAT
A Romantic Comedy

SCREENPLAY

Todd Crawshaw

CrowsnestPublishing.com

Visit: www.toddcrawshaw.com

ISBN-10: 1-7333502-2-5
ISBN-13: 978-1-7333502-2-8

First Edition

Cover design: by author

CrowsnestPublishing.com

Printed in the United States of America

And so castles made of sand,

fall in the sea, eventually.

— *Jimi Hendrix*

ALSO BY TODD CRAWSHAW

God, Sex & Psychosis
a novel

heretofore
a novel

Light-Years in the Dark
storypoems

Exploits of the Satyr
a novel

FADE IN:

INT. A BEDROOM - NIGHT

A BOY, age 12, is sleeping in a bed. A hand comes into view and covers his mouth to muffle his startled CRY.

> HART (V.O.)
> My father had a peculiar way of imparting wisdom. He woke me one night so I'd witness a miracle.

INT. A CAR - NIGHT

The boy shivers, excited. He stares from the passenger seat at his father, smoking a pipe, driving them up a mountain.

> BOY
> I'm not scared.

> FATHER
> It's okay to be scared.

> BOY
> Daniel wasn't scared.

> FATHER
> Is that so.

> BOY
> (thinks)
> Maybe a little.

> FATHER
> In a lion's den? Hell, yes.

> BOY
> An angel protected him.

> FATHER
> I'm no angel, Son.

                    FATHER (cont'd)
               (grins)
          This is more like Abraham taking
          Isaac to the mountain top.

                    BOY
               (deadpan)
          Great. You're going to kill me.
          That's no miracle. You have to part
          the sea or something.

                    FATHER
               (amused)
          You're a weird kid.

EXT. SUMMIT - DAWN

The boy and father watch an orange sunrise upon
the horizon.

                    BOY
          That's not a miracle.

                    FATHER
          That ball of fire could kill you if
          it got any closer. Or decided to
          burst apart and leave us in a wake of
          dust. Show a little respect.

The boys regards the wavering orb.

                    BOY
          That's not going to happen.

                    FATHER
          Someday it will.

The father sucks on his pipe, blows smoke rings
at the sun. The boy expresses disappointment,
but jokes -

                    BOY
          No Santa Claus either, I guess?

                    FATHER
              (smiles)
     From the moment we're born, we're
     ticking time bombs. That light
     empowers us with energy. Feel it?

The boy stops to consider his feelings, kicks the
dirt.

We hear a gentle WIND, then a clock TICKING.

                    BOY
     Some warmth. So what?

                    FATHER
              (relights his pipe)
     That light keeps us in suspense.

The father blows out the match.

                    FATHER
     We're blinded by that star into
     thinking we know what's real.
              (puffs)
     Except we don't. Never have.

                    BOY
              (turns to go)
     Whatever.

                    FATHER
     Don't take my word. Look yourself.

CLOSE on the boy's expression of astonishment and
terror.

Boy's POV: The sun is RED HOT and ENLARGING FAST!

The sun EXPLODES into a tsunami of WHITE LIGHT.

INT. HART'S BEDROOM - NIGHT

A man SHOUTS and lunges forward in bed.

This is ZACHARIUS HART, 36, modestly good-looking
even when disheveled. His face glistens with
sweat in the moonlight.

MIA TAR, 27, naked and pretty, pulls back the
sheets Hart has dislodged from her. She reaches
over and touches him.

>   MIA
> Your chest is wet.

Hart, somewhere in transit, registers her comment.

>   HART
> I was lost at sea.

>   MIA
> Your dad again?

>   HART
> We were watching the sun rise.

>   MIA
> Wonderful. Go back to sleep.

>   HART
> The sun exploded.

>   MIA
> So we died.

>   HART
> Not sure. I woke up.

>   MIA
>   (quips)
> Maybe next time.

Hart settles back onto his pillow and stares at
Mia's face.

>   MIA
> You're getting sleepy, very sleepy.

Hart closes his eyes. A TICKING is heard again.
THE ROOM IGNITES AS IF LIT BY A WHITE-HOT FLARE.

> HART (V.O.)
> Another defining moment. My mother,
> taking me to work. I was nine.

INT. DELIVERY ROOM, HOSPITAL - BRIGHT LIGHTS

We see bassinets, CRYING babies. A nurse dressed in
white holds a baby. Hart's MOTHER, the nurse, beams
with excitement.

Hart is a grownup wearing children's pajamas.

> HART
> Mom? What are you doing here?

> MOTHER
> What do you think I do all day?

> HART
> This can't be real. You're alive.

CLOSE on his fingers checking his wrist for a
pulse.

> HART
> Wait. I can't be dead.

> MOTHER
> You were shot.

> ZACK
> I faked that. I know I did.

He touches his chest. There is blood on his hand.

> MOTHER
> Zacky, you can't fake death.
>   (coos at the baby)
> How do you think these little ones
> get here? They arrive from donors.

5

> MOTHER (cont'd)
> (at her son)
> You don't look pleased.

Hart is panic stricken. His mother is full of bliss.

> MOTHER
> Do you think babies giggle when they
> get yanked from a warm womb? No,
> babies go - wwhhhaaaaaaa!

His mother holds the naked baby upside down by
its legs. She gives its bare bottom a hard SPANK.

> MOTHER
> But you, my little Zacky, you were
> always the exception to the rule.

THE VIEW TURNS 180 DEGREES ON THE BABY'S FACE -
SMILING.

> HART (V.O.)
> She said I laughed when slapped at
> birth. My mom was delusional -

The TICKING gets LOUDER and LOUDER.

> HART (V.O.)
> And bat-shit crazy half the time.

INSERT - RINGING ALARM CLOCK SMASHED TO PIECES WITH
A HAMMER

> HART (V.O.)
> Still, I loved her.

INT. HART'S BEDROOM - DAWN

A hand finds the RINGING alarm. A button pushed.
SILENCE.

> HART (V.O.)
> Zacharius Hart. That's me.

He throws back the bedsheets. He is alone.

                    HART (V.O.)
          I specialize in the abatement of pain
          and suffering. I sell bliss.
                    (yawns)
          I used to be a grief counselor.
          Well, I convinced people I was.

He GROANS at the bright sunlight.

                    HART
          Oh, joy. Another day.

INT. HART'S KITCHEN - DAY

HART, wearing red boxer shorts, pours coffee
beans into a grinder. He regards his reflection
in the window.

                    HART (V.O.)
          Life is not a ticking time bomb.

EXT. HART'S ESTATE - DAY

An aerial view reveals a veranda, pool, gardened
grounds, tennis court, and a three-hole golf
course.

                    HART (V.O.)
          It's a beautiful thing. A gift.
          An atomic bomb, by comparison, is
          insignificant to the radiant powers
          of one good human heart.

The coffee beans GRIND. The grinder DECELERATES.

                    HART (V.O.)
          People tend to trust the physical
          world more than the metaphysical.
                    (beat)
          Take my life.

SERIES OF SHOTS (FLASHBACKS):

HIS FATHER AND MOTHER STARTLED BY A DOORBELL

> HART (V.O.)
> I'm the only child of a radio
> announcer and mostly unemployed
> father and a manic-depressive mom.
> We were constantly on the move.

A DOOR OPENS TO REVEAL A SMILING SALESPERSON

> HART (V.O.)
> But I adapted. From city to city,
> house to house, room to room. To
> avoid process servers.

HART AS A PRE-TEEN BOY STANDING IN DOORWAY

> HART (V.O.)
> I learned to lie with authority.

CLOSEUP ON THE BOY'S STEADFAST DEMEANOR

> BOY
> No. My parents are not at home.

HART AS A TEENAGER AT SCHOOL SURROUNDED BY OTHER KIDS

> HART (V.O.)
> I won over bullies and made friends
> by being a wise-ass with such charm
> even my teachers found me tolerable.

HART, AS A YOUNG ADULT, ON A COLLEGE CAMPUS

> HART (V.O.)
> At colleges I posed as a student,
> attended lectures and interviewed
> professors to learn what I needed to
> about psychology and business.

TWO HANDS HOLD AN UPTURNED AND OPEN PALM

> HART (V.O.)
> When reading palms, skin lines tell
> you nothing. The contact you make by
> touching others is what matters.

HART, AS AN ADULT, SITTING AT A POKER TABLE

> HART (V.O.)
> As in poker, the cards you hold are
> less important than reading your
> opponent's mind, deconstructing their
> body language, and hiding your own
> feelings. That's how you win.

HART AT A PODIUM SPEAKING TO A CAPTIVATED AUDIENCE

> HART (O.C.)
> Alternatively, I am a motivational
> speaker, a man whose words carry more
> confidence than credibility.
> (beat)
> My devoted followers call me Z.

AN ORNATE ENTRY GATE WITH THE WORDS "Z-BLISS" ACROSS

END SERIES OF SHOTS

CLOSE on Hart as he examines his teeth in the
window pane.

> HART (V.O.)
> I'm not a bad person. Not really.

Hart pours a cup of coffee. He hears FOOTSTEPS
and turns.

> HART (V.O.)
> Technically, I've violated no laws.

A damp towel is thrown in his face.

                    HART
     Mia, good morning. I think.

Mia slips a pastel caftan over her swim suit,
assesses his red boxer shorts, before playfully
taking Hart's coffee mug.

                    MIA
     You think? Therefore I am.
          (sips coffee)
     Your devoted fans, they await.

Hart peers through the window, sees people
meandering on the grassy promenade by the pool.
He rehearses his smile in the window pane. He
smiles for Mia who raises an eyebrow.

                    HART
     I need a couple more minutes.

                    MIA
     Your magic powers haven't risen?

                    HART
     I'm fully charged and loaded.

Mia hands back his coffee and kisses him on the cheek.

                    MIA
     Don't waste your mojo on me.

                    HART
     My mojo doesn't rise without you.

                    MIA
     Then I'd better be off to work.

He toasts her with his coffee as she departs.

                    HART (V.O.)
     I once thought happiness was the
     absence of suffering. An uncoupling.
     Separation of incompatible elements.

VIEW OF GOLDEN GATE BRIDGE AND SAN FRANCISCO.

EXT. GOLDEN GATE PARK TRAIL, STOW LAKE - DAY
(FLASHBACK)

                    HART (V.O.)
          Until I met her. Not her. Her.

NATALIE BRIER, 27, is seated on a bench. She is a
force like no other, a transcendental lightning
rod of beauty.

                    HART (V.O.)
          I saw her seated in a park one day.
          Like a delicious problem to surmount.

The sky is overcast with fog. The solitary bench
is beside a path that overlooks a lake. She is
alone. No one else in sight. Her expression is
sad. She projects an aloof gaze.

Hart approaches and seats himself beside her.

                    HART
          You look troubled. Can I help?

She regards his forwardness with suspicion and
sarcasm.

                    NATALIE
          Thanks for noticing my pain.

                    HART
          It's my business to notice these
          things. I'm a grief counselor.

                    NATALIE
          Do I look naive?

He takes out a business card. She peruses,
dismisses it.

11

HART
My friends call me Zack.

NATALIE
How convenient. A friend.

HART
I understand your distrust.

NATALIE
Next you'll want to be my lover.

Hart stands. Apologetic with a bow.

HART
I shouldn't have intruded.

NATALIE
(softly)
No. Stay.

Hart cocks his head, uncertain he's heard her correctly.

NATALIE
(sharper)
Sit.

Hart complies like an obedient dog. He smiles.

HART
Trust me. I won't bite.

Her eyes harbor doubt. But also a delectable allure.

NATALIE
No ulterior motives? Is that what you'd have me believe?

HART
All humans are riddled with flaws.

NATALIE
And I thought you'd be a saint.

The corners of her mouth indicate droll irony,
which appeals to Hart. He waits for her to divulge
her story.

NATALIE
My husband died of a heart attack.

HART
I'm sorry.

NATALIE
On our wedding night. A month ago.

HART
That's terrible.

NATALIE
Yes. I'm grieving, as you can see.

HART
I understand.

NATALIE
No, you don't.

HART
(tries again)
Your husband wouldn't want you to
suffer. He'd want you to move on with
your life and be happy. He's at peace
now. In a better place.

Natalie turns and SLAPS Hart's empathetic
expression away.

NATALIE
How dare you!

Unprepared for this assault, Hart is SLAPPED
again.

                    NATALIE
          Better than this living hell?

Hart stops her hand from striking his face a
third time. There's electricity in their touch.
A beguiling sensuality.

                    NATALIE
          No, you're right. This is not a happy
          place. I wish I was dead.

                    HART
          Don't say that.

                    NATALIE
          Why not? You said so yourself.

                    HART
          Life is precious. It's a gift.

                    NATALIE
          Nonsense. Half the gifts I receive I
          want to exchange.

Hart still holds her hand. She frowns.

                    NATALIE
          What is it with men?

                    HART
          I only want to help.

                    NATALIE
          Even if I killed my husband?

                    HART
          You said he had a heart attack.

                    NATALIE
          People gossip. They say cruel things.

                    HART
Ignore them. It's not uncommon for
the cardiovascular system to fail.

                    NATALIE
So many broken hearts. Why?

                    HART
It's a sad world.

                    NATALIE
He was eighty-one.

                    HART
    Years?

She pulls her hand away.

                    NATALIE
Your expression reminds me of a jury.

                    HART
I wasn't judging.

                    NATALIE
We were having sex.

THE WORD SEX, LIKE A HEX, SCRAMBLES HIS MIND WITH
IMAGES.

                    NATALIE
I'm a hideous spider.

                    HART
Obviously you're not.

She makes a hideous face to self-mock and shock
him.

                    NATALIE
A black widow. That's me.
        (dramatic, maudlin)
I kill every man I've ever loved.

15

                    HART
          That can't be true.

Her hand drifts indecisively. Hart braces for an
assault. Instead she falls into his arms and
SOBS.

                    NATALIE
          My first boyfriend died too.

                    HART
          Died how?

                    NATALIE
          Because of me. I'm lethal. I am.

                    HART
          Wait. Died while having sex?

He attempts to disengage himself, but she pulls
him back.

                    NATALIE
          Hold me tight.

Hart complies. She clings to him. He becomes
aroused by her caress. She pushes away, sits up.
Her moist eyes assess him.

                    NATALIE
          Maybe you're the one.

                    HART
          The one?

                    NATALIE
          Who I've been praying for. To come
          and save me. To break the spell.

                    HART
          What spell?

NATALIE
You'll think I'm mad.

HART
Try me.

NATALIE
My grandmother was clairvoyant. She
told me I'd been cursed by a witch.
For sins committed in my past life.
Only a man who embodies pure love can
save me. But he has to kiss me. Until
then, I kill whoever I fuck.

HART
Seriously?

NATALIE
I know. It sounds stupid.

Not sure what to make of her, he grins.

HART
Well, I did stop to help.

She lifts her arm, touches his cheek. Her hand
recoils. She shuts her eyes and mutters to herself
as if possessed.

NATALIE
I can't. No. I won't. God, stop it.
Just once. Fine. Fuck it. Fuck me.

This turbulent rambling rattles Hart, yet seems to
calm her. She expels a sigh, opens her eyes, and
smiles sadly.

NATALIE
See. I'm damaged goods.

She reaches to explore his face, this time with
both hands.

                    NATALIE
        What the hell. Kiss me. Risk it.

She leans in. They kiss. Hesitantly. Their embrace
turns into passionate kissing. There is fondling.
Unbridled foreplay.

Abruptly she pushes him away and stands, conflicted.

                    NATALIE
        No. You'll end up dead. I wish -

She dashes off like a doomed princess. He is left
speechless, emotionally stirred, his blood and
heart THUMPING.

The THUMBING grows louder and becomes thunderous
APPLAUSE.

INT. AUDITORIUM - NIGHT

An audience is STOMPING, CLAPPING. Hart is at a
lectern.

                    HART
        The supreme enlightenment. Nirvana.
        A state of bliss that is akin to
        well... Yes, making love. Even -

A VISION OF A NAKED NATALIE HALF EXPOSED UNDER
BED SHEETS.

                    HART
        At the risk of dying.

The audience is confused, hands shoot up, lots of
questions.

EXT. HART'S KITCHEN - DAY

Mia holds a carrot stick while listening.

                    HART
     She's unraveling my thoughts, my
     dreams, my speeches. She's forced me
     to reexamine my entire life.

Mia skewers her smile with the carrot, biting off
the tip.

                    MIA
     She took your wallet.

                    HART
     I might have left it at Whole Foods.
     Mia, forget the wallet.

                    MIA
               (like you can)
     Admit it. She mind-fucked you.

                    HART
     No. There was definite chemistry.

                    MIA
     Oh, I can imagine.

                    HART
     That's not how it was, Mia. I'm
     trained at deconstructing people. She
     was clearly... distraught.

                    MIA
     She sounds crazy. Like a fox.

                    HART
     I wasn't mind-fucked. Okay?

                    MIA
               (overly agreeable)
     Okay. I believe you. Better?

EXT. GOLF COURSE, Z-BLISS - DAY

> HART (V.O.)
> No, I was not. I began to doubt
> myself. My purpose. My value.

Surrounding Hart are people seated on a grassy
fairway.

> HART (V.O.)
> I operate a spiritual center which
> provides enlightenment. My critics
> say it's all a scam. A nothingness.
> I desired proof. A true miracle.
> (beat)
> I mean, this world delivers far more
> questions than answers.

INT. LIVING ROOM - NIGHT

Hart and Mia sit beside a fire. Mia holds a BROCHURE.

INSERT - EXTREME NIRVANA: Instant Bliss Designed
for the Insatiable and Privileged Rich.

> MIA
> You can't be serious, Zack.

> HART
> You encouraged me to be.

> MIA
> This is all because of her.

> HART
> This isn't about her.

> MIA
> Okay.

> HART
> She was the catalyst. Granted.

> MIA
> Translation?

                    HART
     It's a new tough-love approach.

                    MIA
     What, a boot camp for nirvana?

EXT. GOLF COURSE FAIRWAY, Z-BLISS - DAY

Hart takes a relaxed practice swing with his
driver. Mia sits in a golf cart watching,
clutching the brochure.

                    MIA
     I hope you know what you're doing.

                    HART
     It's a three-day retreat. In and out.
     What could possibly go wrong?

                    MIA
     You're promising NIRVANA. Zack.

                    HART
     With a money-back guarantee.

                    MIA
     Who in their right mind will fork
     over a quarter million dollars?

                    HART
     Only those who believe money is no
     obstacle. Which is only fair.

                    MIA
     You don't play fair, Zack. What's the
     catch?

Hart smiles, then WHACKS his golf ball off the grass.

                    HART
     I haven't fully worked that out. But
     I'll be debt free if it works.

                    MIA
No one is that stupid to sign up.

INT. HART'S OFFICE, Z-BLISS ESTATE - DAY

                  HART (V.O.)
Then twelve people registered.

Hart reads a news clipping from an opened file in
his lap.

INSERT - NEWS CLIPPING WITH PHOTO AND HIGHLIGHTED
TEXT

                  HART (V.O.)
Russ Field, former CFO of ENROB,
reaped $90 million in compensation
prior to bailing from his executive
duties three months prior to the
energy giant filing for bankruptcy.

Mia snatches the newspaper article from Hart's
hands.

CLOSE on a smiling executive being escorted by
police and lawyers from a highrise through a
throng of reporters.

                  MIA (V.O.)
It's nice to know the people he
screwed are financing his salvation.

                  HART (V.O.)
I accessed his flight schedule and
reserved you a seat. Check him out.

INT. COMMERCIAL AIRPLANE, FIRST CLASS - NIGHT

RUSS FIELD, 55, who resembles a famous actor, is
sitting by the window trying to be inconspicuous.
He talks softly into a cell phone while staring
into the blackness outside.

                    FIELD
Unsubstantiated. Alleged. No, not
true. There's no substantiated proof.

He notices the reflection of a pretty face, MIA,
the woman seated next to him. Clearly she's
eavesdropping.

                    FIELD
Excuse me. This is private.

                    MIA
Then I'd advise using the toilet.

                    FIELD
         (at the phone)
Nobody. Listen, Darling... Beth. Hear
me out. No laws were broken. No, yes,
that's right... this Grand Jury thing
is merely a formality.
         (bolder)
Yes, I am innocent. I can't believe
you'd think. Yes, of course. That's
right. A scapegoat. Exactly.

He smiles, reaching an even keel, then loses his
temper.

                    FIELD
Oh, for fuck-sake! Can't you ever -
Jesus, Beth! I'm the one who needs
the god-damned peace and quiet right
now! I'm under tremendous stress!

A STEWARDESS approaches from behind a curtain on
the plane.

                    FIELD
Beth? Hello? Are you there?

                    STEWARDESS
Sir, I must insist you refrain from -

                    FIELD
Absolutely right. My language? Bad
form. It won't happen again.

                  STEWARDESS
Oh, my god!

                    MIA
              (startled)
What?

                  STEWARDESS
Nothing. Not you. It's -
              (at Field)
Oh, my god, it is you.

Field reacts with semi-alarm. He's uncertain to
whom she's referring to - his true self or fake
celebrity self.

                    FIELD
              (enigmatic smile)

                  STEWARDESS
Your secret is safe. Harrison Ford
was on my last flight.

The stewardess zips her lips and smiles.

                  STEWARDESS
Can I get you a complementary drink?

                    FIELD
              (relieved)
Desperate for one. Vodka on ice.

                  STEWARDESS
              (at Mia)
And you, Miss?

                    MIA
The same. And orange juice.

Field pockets his phone, gives Mia a dose of fulsome charm.

                    FIELD
    Not strictly true. It's not the same.

                    MIA
    Excuse me?

                    FIELD
    A screw driver. You asked for one.

                    MIA
    Are you a celebrity?

                    FIELD
    What if I told you I was?

                    MIA
    I'd require substantiated proof.

                    FIELD
    Touché.

INT. PLASTIC SURGERY RECOVERY ROOM - DAY

Two woman, both 30, Suzzie and Michelle, are seated next to one another, holding mirrors. Their faces are swollen red.

                    SUZZIE
          (moans)
    This is awful. We're ugly.

                    MICHELLE
    It's the price you pay for beauty.
    Skin peels are revitalizing.

                    SUZZIE
    I look like a peeled plum.

INT. COMMERCIAL AIRPLANE, FIRST CLASS - SAME NIGHT

RUSS FIELD, now drunk, toasts MIA with a smile of regret.

> RUSS
> Married. I'll be getting a divorce.

> MIA
> Lucky you. What's in Wyoming?

> RUSS
> I'm attending an exclusive retreat.

> MIA
> What are you retreating from?

> RUSS
> Nothing. It's a vacation. A quarter of a million dollar vacation.

> MIA
> Wow. You must be really...

He smugly waits for her praise.

> MIA
> Desperate to escape.

INT. HILLER RESIDENCE, GAME ROOM - DAY

Seated at his bar, HAROLD HILLER, 45, removes his glasses, rubs his eyes. He looks around holding a glass of whiskey. He squints, attaches his glasses, meanders along the walls.

CLOSE on a photo of him shaking hands with Trump, another meeting Reagan, along with a sundry of other politicians.

Hiller stops again, sips his whiskey. His jaw lifts, his muscles tense. Tears form and trickle from his eyes.

CLOSE on a handsome young man holding a
football. His other arm is clasped around a
proud man, Hiller.

INSERT - A FRAMED QUOTATION NEXT TO THE PHOTO:

> I am living proof of my father.
> And now he is living through me.
> - Howard Hiller

CLOSE on Hiller finishing his whiskey. His hand
shakes. His fingers squeeze hard - HARDER. Then
he empties the glass.

                    HILLER
          Steady soldier. Steady.

He backs away and grips the pool table for
support.

                    HILLER
          Jesus Christ. Jesus H. Christ!!!

He hurls the glass. It SHATTERS against the
wall. Regaining control, he removes his glasses,
wipes his eyes.

                    DOROTHY
          Harold! What happened?

                    HILLER
          Nothing! What's taking you so long?

                    DOROTHY
          It certainly sounded like something.

                    HILLER
          I broke a damned glass! Do a Hail
          Mary or whatever it takes. Can you be
          on time for once in your life?

He moves toward a painting of Jesus hung from
the crucifix. He halfheartedly crosses himself.

He flips back the hinged reproduction where a
safe is kept, turns the combination.

Hiller takes out a gun. He stuffs it inside a
duffle bag. Closing the safe, he frowns at the
Savior's sorrowful eyes.

> HILLER
> Don't give me that look. Where the
> hell were you? I don't have time for
> this right now.

> DOROTHY
> Harold, are they here?

> HILLER
> No. They haven't arrived yet.

> DOROTHY
> Then who are you talking to?

> HILLER
> (at Jesus)
> Nobody.

INT. HART'S OFFICE, Z-BLISS ESTATE - DAY

Hart is rummaging through several files on his desk.

PHOTOS OF TWO UNATTRACTIVE WOMAN MARKED "BEFORE"

> HART
> Socialites. Both inherited fortunes
> from generous fathers.

> MIA
> Also their unremarkable looks.

PHOTOS TWO ATTRACTIVE WOMAN MARKED "AFTER"

> MIA
> I see they worship regularly at the
> church of plastic surgery.

28

INT. AIRPORT RESTAURANT, REST ROOM - NIGHT

The same two women, resembling Barbie Dolls,
stand side-by-side, facing a wall mirror.

MICHELE applies lipstick with the skill of a
surgeon. SUZZIE brushes on eye shadow.

> SUZZIE
> I look in a mirror each day just to
> convince myself I still exist.

Michele, attending to herself, barely registers
the remark.

> MICHELE
> What are you talking about?

> SUZZIE
> I can hardly believe what I see.

> MICHELE
> Suzzie, you're talking nonsense.

> SUZZIE
> Are we pretty on the inside too?

> MICHELE
> You're talking like an idiot.

> SUZZIE
> Being grounded. I'm talking about Z.

> MICHELE
> Now you're talking about an idiot.

> SUZZIE
> He is not, Mickey. I worship him.

Suzzie holsters her lipstick with a professional
SNAP-CLICK.

                    MICHELE
You do need grounding. That's the
only reason I agreed to come along.

                    SUZZIE
Z is so wise, like a god.

                    MICHELE
A man who wears a full length dress?

                    SUZZIE
It's a transcendental robe.

                    MICHELE
Close enough.

INT. HART'S OFFICE, Z-BLISS ESTATE - DAY

Mia, on a tennis court, hands Hart another file.

                    HART
          (brightens)
Dorothy. One of my biggest fans.
She's been a generous supporter.
          (darkens)
Coming with husband. Who I haven't
met. Hum, real estate developer.

                    MIA
Their son died. A year ago. He was
twenty-one. Killed himself during
spring break. Overdosed. College.

                    HART
She's talked about him a lot.

INT. HELICOPTER, HILLER'S RESIDENCE - DAY

Seated behind the PILOT is Harold Hiller and his
wife, DOROTHY, 39. She gazes vacantly ahead at
the horizon while Hiller holds and pats the
small bag in his lap.

                    PILOT
We'll be there in an hour, tops.
Weather's clear. Enjoy the ride.

                    DOROTHY
          (as if awakening)
I'm sorry, what did he say, Dear?

                    HILLER
Jesus, I'm beginning to think your
mind has already left us.

                    DOROTHY
          (confused)
Why would he think that, Harold?

                    HILLER
Not the pilot. I'm saying it.

                    DOROTHY
I'm so glad you decided to come. It's
peaceful. I feel Matthew's presence
each time I'm there.

                    HAROLD
          (scoffs)
All because of this Z character.

                    DOROTHY
Z will help you find your bliss.

The pilot starts the ENGINE and gives a backward
glance.

Hiller glares back for him to mind his own
business.

                    HAROLD
I highly doubt it.
          (grimaces)
It's not scientifically possible.

                    DOROTHY
The veil of time is removed. And you
find you're in a beautiful realm.

                    HAROLD
Yeah, for Z. That bastard bilked us
out of hundreds of thousands -

                    DOROTHY
All proceeds benefit the Foundation
for the Preservation of Bliss.

                    HAROLD
Wow. He sounds like a real prince.

                    DOROTHY
        (shuts her eyes)
Harold, you have so much negative
energy. I worry about you.

                    HAROLD
Well don't.

                    DOROTHY
Be a vessel for goodness.

                    HAROLD
Jesus Christ, Dorothy, you should
listen to yourself sometimes.

The helicopter LIFTS off into the blue sky.

INT. LIVING ROOM, Z-BLISS ESTATE - NIGHT

Mia hands Hart a ROLLING STONE magazine.

THE COVER SHOWS A PUNK-ROCK BAND WITH THE HEADLINE:

            Has PISS Lost Its
            Caustic Vigor?
            Clean and Straight Out
            of Rehab!

INT. MUSIC RECORDING STUDIO - DAY

PISS, a band composed of ZIT, NED, JED, JOE,
listen to their manager, BRADY, as they PLUCK and
TAP their instruments.

                    BRADY
          Boo-hoo, boys. Whine all you want
          about how you've all bloody suffered.
          Been a fun ride into the gutter,
          hasn't it lads? Now you're sober.
          Frightening, ain't it? 'Cause I got
          another bloody wake-up call for ya.

Brady hands the band members financial
statements. Each one gazes at the figures as if
at hieroglyphics.

                    BRADY
          PISS is in financial decline. Album
          sales down. Meaning, you don't suck
          the knobs of the corporate heads and
          satisfy 'em with a hit single pronto
          - you'll be more 'an washed up.

His pep talk fails to stir them into decisive
action.

                    ZIT
          Speak English, Brady.

                    BRADY
          You'll be washing dishes, lads.

                    JOE
          Dishes?

                    ZIT
          The fuck we will.

                    BRADY
          Platinum days are over. Millions got
          flushed through your bloody veins.

                    BRADY (cont'd)
              (nasty wink)
      Thank me later for saving your asses.

                      JED
      Watcha chewing, Brady?

                      ZIT
      Spit it out already.

Brady holds a brochure. The musicians stir with
interest.

                     BRADY
      Extreme Nirvana. It's a retreat.

                      ZIT
      The hell's this?

                      NED
      You want us to surrender?

                     BRADY
      Exclusive mind-altering workshop. At
      a quarter million per head.

                      JOE
      Piss off, Brady.

                      NED
      You're in your cups, man.

                      JED
      Yeah, drink my piss. Bottoms up!

The lads LAUGH. Tolerating their foul humor, Brady displays a smile that would kill if it could. He explains -

                     BRADY
      It's a publicity stunt. A haven for
      you to restore your juices. Complete
      a song. You notify me, I alert the
      media. It'll be a bloody coup.

                    ZIT
In proper English, Brady.

                    BRADY
          (gestures)
Breaking News: PISS Raises Hell At Z-
Bliss! Be nice. Then create a ruckus.
Your reputation gets restored to its
original brand of tarnished luster.

                    JED
You're mad.

                    ZIT
Four of us? That's one million!

                    NED
Ain't piss'n' me money on 'at.

                    BRADY
Ah, there's a moneyback guarantee.
Trust me, lads, this is a win-win.

INT. CNN CORPORATE OFFICE, CONFERENCE ROOM - DAY

WILL SAVAGE, 37, sits with the EDITOR-IN-CHIEF,
EXECUTIVES and ATTORNEY who mutter as they peruse
the Z-Bliss brochure.

BROCHURE COVER: EXTREME NIRVANA: Instant Bliss
Designed...

                    EDITOR-IN-CHIEF
Where did you get this?

                    SAVAGE
Exclusive mailing. Only the wealthy
few receive it. I have my sources.

                    EDITOR-IN-CHIEF
How can anyone claim to guarantee
nirvana? This is preposterous.

All LAUGH in agreement. Savage SLAPS a report on
the table.

                    SAVAGE
        A charlatan. He calls himself Z and
        conducts spiritual retreats. A guru
        who claims to deliver enlightenment.
        Guru, my ass.

Everyone begins to take interest.

                    EXECUTIVE
        We know your distaste for all things
        fraudulent, Will.

                    SAVAGE
        I want to expose this bastard.

                    EDITOR-IN-CHIEF
        By paying him a quarter million?
            (scowls)
        So you can tear off his wings?

                    SAVAGE
        The brochure guarantees satisfaction.
        Or a refund. It's a legal document.

                    EDITOR-IN-CHIEF
        And what if you do achieve nirvana?

Everyone LAUGHS but Savage.

                    SAVAGE
        I've debunked charlatans before.
        Fraudulent corporations. All types of
        deceptive partnerships.

                    EXECUTIVE
        Including cheating spouses?

                    ATTORNEY
        I heard you planted bugs around the
        house and video recorded your wife.

                    SAVAGE
              (sour smile)
I get results. I succeed, gentlemen.

                   EXECUTIVE
Doing it with her yoga instructor?

                 EDITOR-IN-CHIEF
Pilates. A personal trainer.

                    SAVAGE
I do whatever it takes to expose the
truth, no matter how much it hurts.

                 EDITOR-IN-CHIEF
A quarter million. That hurts.

                    SAVAGE
An exclusive story. Ratings will
soar. It'll generate huge revenues.

                 EDITOR-IN-CHIEF
You're quite the gambler, Will.
              (rubs thumb and finger)
With other people's money.

                    SAVAGE
Chief, this man's not only a danger
to society but an insult to religion.

His boss SNORTS and LAUGHS.

                 EDITOR-IN-CHIEF
Will, coming from you, that's funny
- being a devout atheist!

EXT. SWIMMING POOL, Z-BLISS ESTATE - DAY 1

Hart sits in a lounge chair wearing a swim suit
looking tan and fit. Mia, in a bikini, lounges
nearby with a daiquiri in one hand, a file in
another, which she hands to him.

PHOTO OF WILL SAVAGE AND HIS PROFILE HISTORY

                    HART
        This man's not a happy camper.

                    MIA
        Employed by CNN. He registered under
        a ficticious name: Will Melior. The
        man is coming here to destroy you.

                    HART
        I'd be disappointed if he didn't try.
             (shuts file)
        What did you make of Russ Field?

                    MIA
        Handsome. Lacks charm. In denial.

She hands him another file and takes a sip of her
daiquiri.

                    HART
        Who's this?

                    MIA
        Number eleven and twelve. Melvin
        Tobin and guest.

Hart widens his eyes, WHISTLES and flips open the
file.

INSERT - PHOTO OF MELVIN TOBIN AND PAGES OF
INFORMATION

                    HART (V.O.)
        This is a major catch. Boy wonder and
        founder of InnerChip. Nice.

                    MIA
        He could bring unwanted attention.

Hart flips nonchalantly through Tobin's profile.

                    HART
He's discrete. Who's number twelve?

                    MIA
Tobin didn't disclose his guest.

Mia is busy smearing sunscreen on her tanned skin.

                    HART
That was a requirement.

                    MIA
For a quarter million? He could bring
his pet poodle for all I care.

                    HART
I care.

                    MIA
Because you're anal.

                    HART
It's important for my research.

                    MIA
To prove what again?

Mia reclines, turns over on her stomach, unhooks
her bra.

                    MIA
Do my back?

Hart sets down the files. He rubs lotion on her.

                    HART
I want to discover what makes us
tick. Deep down, that mortal coil.

Mia moans pleasurably.

                    MIA
I think you found it.

                    HART
        Something deeper.

                    MIA
        Plumb deeper, I'm willing.

Hart stops massaging and sits back in his chair.

                    HART
        Our guests are due to arrive.

                    MIA
        You haven't plumbed me in weeks. Is
        there somebody else?

                    HART
        It's not what you think.

                    MIA
        Meaning?

                    HART
        I've gone celibate, for awhile.

                    MIA
        Well, great. Go fuck yourself.

She GIGGLES impishly. She feigns modesty,
fastening her top.

                    HART
        You could sue for sexual harassment.

                    MIA
        I would if this was a real job.

She watches him as he reads.

                    MIA
        Keep looking, but you won't find your
        soul inside any of these people.

EXT. CIRCULAR DRIVEWAY, Z-BLISS ESTATE - DAY 1

Guests arrive by limousine. Their bags are removed
by male assistants - ZEKE, JAKE, JESS - who are
large and muscular, wearing black robes. They are
mute, attentive, intimidating.

By contrast, Mia, wearing a bright ceremonial
gown, greets each attendee with effervescence
and devotional pomp.

> HART (V.O.)
> Uncover what you can on this guest of
> Tobin's. Number twelve.

> MIA (V.O.)
> Your 12th disciple?

INT. LIVING ROOM, Z-BLISS ESTATE - DAY 1

The guests awkwardly mingle. Platters of
vegetables are on a table. Savage picks up
celery and says to Field -

> SAVAGE
> Not even fresh. Hey, aren't you -

Field is quick with a preemptive handshake and
greeting -

> FIELD
> I'm Russ. You?

> SAVAGE
> Will.

> FIELD
> (at Suzzie)
> She says the place has a labyrinth.

> SUZZIE
> Z's topiary garden. Wait until you
> experience it. The maze is fun.

FIELD
Let's explore this maze together.
I've been told I'm quite the bull.

CLOSE on Suzzie's and Michele's polite frozen
smiles.

The members of PISS sit in a group, wearing jeans,
leather jackets, tattoos, piercings. They sneer,
reverse snobbery.

HILLER
No dress requirement, I see.

DOROTHY
Harold, your manners.

MELVIN TOBIN arrives last, and alone. He appears
lost, an introvert catapulted into an unwanted
celebrity status.

HILLER
That's Melvin Tobin!

INT. LIVING ROOM, Z-BLISS ESTATE - AN HOUR LATER

The guests are seated, fidgeting, getting anxious,
angry. Tobin keeps to himself, meandering by the
food table. Hiller approaches and extends his hand
to be shaken by Tobin.

HILLER
Harold Hiller. You've probably heard
of me. You're Melvin Tobin.

Tobin nods evasively and extends his hand before
realizing he holds a limp carrot and declines to
shake hands.

HILLER
Thank God you're here. I thought I'd
be surrounded by total lunatics!

INT. LIVING ROOM, Z-BLISS ESTATE - THREE HOURS LATER

Guests are seated, others standing, pacing.
Hiller glares at his wrist watch, at his wife,
at Tobin.

                    HILLER
          No one keeps me waiting this long.
          We're leaving. Dorothy -

                    HART
          Good day, or rather, good evening.

Hart stands in a doorway, dressed in a robe, his
arms spread.

                    HART
          You've had time, I hope, to get to
          know your fellow attendees.

                    HILLER
          You kept us waiting. For three hours.

                    HART
          And yet you opted not to leave.

Hiller glances around for moral support.

                    HART
          Let me show you your accommodations.

The attendees follow Hart toward the veranda.

                    HILLER
               (mutters)
          This had better be first class.

EXT. 1ST FAIRWAY, Z-BLISS ESTATE - LATER

The guests, dumfounded, stare at a groomed fairway
of dewy grass and an assortment of tents and
porta-potties.

                    HILLER
You have got to be shitting me. I
didn't pay a fortune so I could camp
out on your god-damned property!

                    HART
That's precisely what you did. Mia.

                    SUZZIE
What about the ashram huts?

                    HART
Not this time, Suzzie.

                    SUZZIE
But I told Mickey we —

Mia arrives wearing a white bedsheet, resembling
a poncho tied at the waist, and rubber sandals.
She has a stack of more sandals and bedsheets.

                    HART
During your stay you'll wear these.

                    SAVAGE
Is this a joke?

                    HART
Or nothing. Your choice.

                    FIELD
I won't. It's... undignified.

                    HART
Dignity. Yes, we work on that here.

Mia passes out the bedsheets and hands one to
Russ Field.

                    FIELD
Wait. I can't believe it's you.

MIA
Yes, me. Mia. Hello again.

FIELD
Why are you here?

MIA
(winks)
In search of a rich husband.

HILLER
I am not wearing a god-damn dress!

HART
Think of it as a robe.

HILLER
Horseshit.

HART
Thank you. Over there are your porta-
potties. You'll be provided only the
basics during your stay.

Michele and Suzzie express simultaneous alarm.

SUZZIE
But our luggage.

MICHELE
Our makeup.

BOTH WOMEN
We need them.

HART
Confiscated. To achieve nirvana.

TOBIN
No internet?

HART
No exceptions. If you want nirvana.

                    HILLER
I want my god-damn money back.

                    HART
After you've endured my 3-day retreat
and determine the results are not to
your liking.

                    HILLER
I am going to sue your ass.

Hiller grabs his wife by the arm.

                    HILLER
Where are my bags! We're leaving.

                    DOROTHY
            (not budging)
No, Harold, we are not leaving.

                    HILLER
            (overriding her)
We are. Now!

                    DOROTHY
You go. I'm staying.

                    HILLER
Can't you see this is insane?

                    SAVAGE
I can.

                    HILLER
            (points)
This man is a lunatic. A fraud. He's
playing us all for fools!

                    SAVAGE
            (encourages)
Here! Here!

                    HART
I have promised you will achieve
nirvana and I intend on delivering.
For those who are willing to stay.

                  DOROTHY
I'm willing, Z.

                   HILLER
Dorothy. Listen to yourself.

                   SUZZIE
I too am willing.

                  MICHELE
Suzzie!

The members of PISS give a thumb-and-pinky-finger
salute.

                    ZIT
Piss is in. Naked if ya want.

                    HART
Your choice.

                   TOBIN
No electronics. At all?

                    HART
Not this time, Melvin. You paid for a
guest. What happened? A no-show?

                   TOBIN
        (crestfallen)
My fiancé decided not to come.

                    HART
Transcendence is a hard sell.

                   TOBIN
That's the strange thing. She was the
one who suggested we sign up.

>   FIELD
> I'd like to complain about the food.

Hart puts a finger to his lips, then his palms
together.

>   HART
> Choose a tent. Pair up. Select a
> partner. Mia has distributed your
> sandals and bedsheets. There's rope
> provided. It can be used as a belt.

>   SAVAGE
> Or noose.

>   HART
> Optional. Mia will collect your
> clothing. I'll see you bright and
> early. When the rooster crows.

>   MICHELE
> What about our undergarments?

>   HART
> Optional. Good night.

>   HILLER
>   (enraged)
> This is not what I signed up for!

>   HART
> Then a driver will escort you home.
>   (bows)
> And thank you for your donation.

>   HILLER
> Wait just a god-damned minute!

Hiller approaches Hart but is stopped by JAKE
and DEKE.

                    HILLER
    Your bodyguards? I can see why you
    need them. All right, goddamn it.
    I'll stay, for now. You win.

                    HART
    Nothing lost. Nothing gained.

Dorothy hugs her husband.

                    DOROTHY
    Thank you for staying, Harold.

INT. KITCHEN, Z-BLISS ESTATE - NIGHT

Hart and Mia face each other across a table eating
ice cream.

                    MIA
    You've entered dangerous territory.

Hart flashes her an ambivalent smile.

                    MIA
    These are powerful people who can,
    and will, crush you financially.

                    HART
    I've calculated the risks.

INT. DEKE'S BEDROOM, Z-BLISS ESTATE - NIGHT

The three bodyguards, Deke, Jake, Jess, stand facing
a television as they pump iron, curling dumb bells.

EXT. VERANDA AND POOL, Z-BLISS - SUNRISE - DAY 2

A rooster is heard CROWING.

Mia pushes a console button. A musical REVEILLE
in a mix of polka-rock-opera BLARES from
speakers. Hart stands on a promenade overlooking
1st fairway. He holds a megaphone.

> HART (O.C.)
> Awake! Time for karma cleansing!

EXT. 1ST FAIRWAY, Z-BLISS ESTATE - DAY 2

Wearing bedsheets, the attendees emerge from
their tents.

EXT. 1ST TEE - DAY 2

The breakfast buffet is on tables. There is
bottled water. Paper bowls hold granola, nuts,
and fruit. No utensils. Hart arrives eating a
pastry and drinking a cup of coffee.

Savage, smoking a cigarette, approachs Hart.

> SAVAGE
> Where's the Danish and coffee?

Hart swallows the last bite. From Savage's mouth
he plucks the cigarette, takes a puff, then
tosses it to the grass.

> HART
> No smoking. No coffee. No pastries.
> Not if you want nirvana.

Hart looks up into the cloudless sky and announces -

> HART
> It's going to be a hot one. I'd
> advise you drink lots of liquid.

EXT. 1ST GREEN - DAY 2 - MORNING

Troubled by Hart's unorthodox methods, the
attendees stir. Seated in a circle around the
flag in its pin, each one of the attendees holds
a mirror with a crack in the glass.

Hiller refuses to sit, but is coaxed down by the
others.

>   HART (O.C.)
> What we do today will seem crazy. We
> will begin stripping the gears of
> habitual behavior to prepare you for
> a later flight into the inner cosmos.
> This mantra has no meaning, but -
>   (inhales, exhales)
> Negates your negative thoughts:
> I-diot-I-diot-I-diot-I-diot-I-diot-

CLOSE on HILLER'S scowling face in his broken
mirror.

EXT. SAND TRAP BY 2ND HOLE - DAY 2 - LATE MORNING

Field is standing, his back to Hart, whose arms
are held out to catch him. Field lets go,
falling backward as Hart turns away, distracted
by a woman walking toward them.

NATALIE BRIER. She is blasé, arriving fashion-
ably late.

Field lands on his back with a THUD in the sand
trap.

>   FIELD
> You bastard! You tricked me!

>   HART
> That was deliberate. An important
> lesson. Know who to trust.

All heads turn to Natalie as she nears. She is
wearing sun glasses, a silk blouse, leather
pants, and pumps.

>   SUZZIE
> What is she doing here?

>   NATALIE
> What have I missed?

51

                    TOBIN
     Marvelous, you made it! Everyone,
     this is my fiancé, Natalie.

The men gawk, also embarrassed to be wearing
bedsheets.

                    MICHELE
     You can't be dressed like that.

                    SUZZIE
     Those are the rules.

                    NATALIE
                 (at Hart)
     You must be Z.

Hart, astounded that it's her, recovers and nods.

                    HART
     Right. Suzzie's correct. You must
     wear a bedsheet for this retreat.

                    NATALIE
     Do I undress here?

Kicking off her shoes, she begins unbuttoning
her blouse.

                    HART
     Mia will see that you get a sheet and
     show you where to change. Mia?

Mia, observing, is seated on a knoll and rises.

                    MIA
     This way, Ms ... ?

Natalie removes her sunglasses.

                    NATALIE
     Brier. Natalie. And you?

                    MIA
Mia.

                  NATALIE
Pretty name. Where to, Mia?

                  SAVAGE
You look familiar.

                  NATALIE
I often get that. I don't know why.
        (at Hart)
As do you. Look familiar.

                   HART
I get that too.

EXT. BUFFET LUNCH, 1ST GREEN - DAY 2

On tables are paper bags. Inside are McDonald's
Happy Meals. The attendees rummage and discover
cold burgers and fries. Hiller finds a plastic
toy, a cow, with words imprinted:

INSCRIPTION - "HOLY COW, I GOT MILKED!"

Hiller throws down his lunch.

                  HILLER
This is outrageous!

                   HART
Problems?

                  HILLER
I'm tired of your insults.

                   HART
Nap time in ten minutes.

Hiller moves toward Hart. Dorothy moves between
them.

                    DOROTHY
It's only a toy. Have mine, it's
blue, not pink.

                    HILLER
I don't want your cow. I want him to
explain the meaning of this!

                    HART
The meaning will come in time.

Hart's sheet is colorfully tie-dyed. His hands
rise, palms pressed together, as a sign of peace.

                    HILLER
And your 3-hole golf course, which my
money helped pay for, how does that
equate with attaining nirvana?

                    HART
A good question. To suffer is the
path to nirvana. When I make a bad
putt, it helps me suffer.

Hillers breaks from his wife's restraining grip
but stops.

                    HILLER
You know nothing about suffering.

Natalie now wears a white sheet tied at her waist
with rope. She takes an inquisitive bite from her
burger, sets it down.

                    MICHELE
Excuse me, Z, I'm a vegetarian.

                    SUZZIE
We both are.

                         HART
Try the fries.

                    TOBIN
Everything is cold and soggy.

The members of PISS sit on the grass devouring
their meals.

                    NED
Quit bitch'n, man. It's food.

                    HART
          (salutes them)
Clearly on their way to nirvana.

Tobin sits on the grass beside Natalie. Her hand
slides to his thigh. He squeamishly evades this
public intimacy.

                    TOBIN
Where's your engagement ring?

                    NATALIE
I was told to remove everything.

                    TOBIN
You mean...

                    DOROTHY
Dear, your underwear is allowed.

Natalie bites her lip, gives a sideways glance
at Mia.

                    NATALIE
Oops. Apparently I misunderstood.

Tobin transfers his annoyance to the food being
offered. He notices Natalie is not eating. He
says to Hart -

                    TOBIN
Respectfully, Z, I have to say, I
don't understand the point of this.

                    HART
That is the point you must ponder.
And ponder you will after your one
hour nap. While I go have a swim.

                    HILLER
Jesus-H-Christ. He's treating us like
we're back in kindergarten.

Hart turns to leave and Natalie says to him -

                    NATALIE
Nice circus. What time do we eat fire
and swallow swords?

EXT. SWIMMING POOL - DAY 2

Hart surfaces, climbs from the pool. He sits
beside Mia.

                    MIA
What are you doing?

                    HART
What do you think I'm doing?

                    MIA
          (testy)
Don't play that game with me.

                    HART
I told you, I'm experimenting.

                    MIA
To see who will kill you first?

                    HART
          (mock concern)
Should I have factored that in?

                    MIA
How do you know her?

                    HART
Who?

                    MIA
You know who. Tobin's guest.

                    HART
We met. Once.

                    MIA
(realizing)

                    HART
Mia, I swear, I had no idea.

                    MIA
I have intel on her. Interested?

INT. HART'S STUDY - DAY 2

Hart holds printouts. Mia sits on the corner of
his desk.

INSERT - NEWS ARTICLE AND PHOTOS OF NATALIE

                    MIA
Her hubby did die. On the wedding
night. No proof of foul play.

                    HART
What about the others?

                    MIA
What others?

She pulls another page from a folder.

                    MIA
The husband had no living relatives
to dispute the will. She's smart.

                    HART
She's a little vixen.

                         MIA
        Maybe you've met your match.

Mia's smile is laden with sarcasm.

                         HART
        You doubt her innocence.

                         MIA
        Inherited a fortune. Her hubby was
        eighty-something. And she was, what,
        in her teens. No, twenties.
                (jeers)
        Why would I doubt her innocence?

                         HART
        I think you admire her.

                         MIA
        Sure. She's devious.
                (slides off the desk)
        We need to know her game plan.

                         HART
        Landing the big fish. Tobin.

                         MIA
        Too simple.

                         HART
        You're ruling out true love?

                         MIA
        Don't be stupid.
                (beat)
        She came here after you.

EXT. 2ND FAIRWAY - DAY 2 - AFTERNOON

The attendees are lying on the grass. Tobin is
whispering to Natalie as he holds her hand.
Hiller is asleep, SNORING vociferously. The
members of PISS sit by themselves.

                    ZIT
          Any bright ideas, mates?

                    JED
          I could use a bloody fix.

The others pounce on him. Zit SLAPS him, twists an
ear.

                    ZIT
          No fix! We're all in a fix.

                    NED
          Stay clean. We stay together.

                    JED
          They took our guitars!

                    JOE
          No strings, no bloody song.

                    JED
          Brady, he expects to be rung.

                    ZIT
          So we hum out a tune, add words.

                    JED
          We've never sung in our lives.

                    JOE
          We shout and scream.

                    ZIT
          Bloody hell.

Hart returns to the grassy knoll with twelve women
resembling nurses in white uniforms and his staff
- Zeke, Jake, Jess.

                    HART
          I trust you had refreshing naps.

Hiller wakes with a SNORT and fumbles to find his glasses. Suzzie and Michele are picking grass off each other like grooming primates. Savage stands, alerted, seeing the nurses.

> SAVAGE
> Now what?

> HART
> A hot mud bath. Cleanses the pores.

> ZIT
> Bloody hell.

EXT. PUTTING GREEN - DAY 2 - AFTERNOON

The attendees are herded along, guided by the nurses and bodyguards toward a cluster of thatched huts.

> SUZZIE
> There. The ashram huts I told you about. Aren't they pretty, Mickey?

> MICHELE
> Coming here was a bad idea.

> SUZZIE
> Mud baths are purifying.

> MICHELE
> I'm already a hot mess.

Hiller, Savage, and Field walk in loose single file. They give dagger looks at Hart. He salutes them as they pass.

> HART
> Cheer up. We meet afterward at the veranda bar for shots of tequila.

Hiller stops abruptly. Savage and Field BUMP into him.

                    HILLER
It's a mud bath. Why the nurses?

                    HART
Mud. Shower. Massage. Enema.

                    SAVAGE
Enema?

                    HART
Highly cleansing.

                    HILLER
No thanks. Is drinking tequila what
you call achieving nirvana?

                    HART
No, I call it Happy Hour.

EXT. VERANDA BAR - DAY 2 - DUSK

The attendees line the bar. Multiple shot
glasses are full of tequila. Hart, behind the
bar, holds a glass aloft -

                    HART
Salute!

                    FIELD
To what?

                    HART
Blowing off useless carbon.

Savage downs his glass and grabs for another.

                    SAVAGE
I'll drink to that.

EXT. VERANDA BAR - DAY 2 - NIGHT

The woman are together, the men in their own

group, except for Tobin and Natalie who sit by
themselves at a table.

                    TOBIN
        Natalie, you don't realize ... how
        much I ... I am... really wasted.
                (blinks)
        How I adore you.

                    NATALIE
        You're so sexy in that dress.

CLOSE on Tobin's bedsheet, showing he has an erection.

                    NATALIE
        You've made a little tent for me.

                    TOBIN
                (embarrassed)
        I'm so happy you changed your mind
        and decided to come. But frankly, the
        methods he's employing, I -

                    NATALIE
        Forget that.

                    TOBIN
        You're ... God ... so beautiful.

                    NATALIE
        Am I?

                    TOBIN
        Compared to me, I'm not, you know.

                    NATALIE
        You're shy. I find that attractive.

                    TOBIN
        You do?

                    NATALIE
        I do.

The members of PISS have teamed up to challenge
Savage, Field, Hiller in a drinking match. They
consume drink for drink as Suzzie, Michele and
Dorothy cheer them on.

                    WOMEN
          Blah-Blah-Blah! Piss-Boom-Baw!

                    ZIT
               (downs a shot)
          Match that!

                    FIELD
          Liquid's gonna start squirting from
          all your pierced holes.

                    SAVAGE
          Good one, Russ.

                    ZIT
          You ain't even in our league, man.

                    NED
          Our band, we been there and back.

                    SAVAGE
          And where is there?

                    ZIT
          Pissing gutter, man.

                    JED
          PISS is back! United we stand!

                    FIELD
          And fall if you stand.

                    SAVAGE
          Hey, where's our nirvana leader?

Hiller looks around, adjusts his glasses, leans
into the group and BLURTS in a LOUD false whisper.

                    HILLER
          Listen, next time he asks us to hop
          like a bunny, I say we kill him.

There is raucous LAUGHTER.

EXT. BALCONY - DAY 2 - NIGHT

Hart and Mia listen from above on a balcony.

                     MIA
          Happy now? They're all conspiring to
          kill you.

                    HART
          It's merely a release of tension.

                     MIA
          Oh, please. They're plastered.

                    HART
          Aren't you fascinated by this?

                     MIA
          I'm going inside. Do you need me?

Hart vacantly shakes his head. He's watching Natalie.

                     MIA
          I didn't think so.

EXT. VERANDA - LATER

CLOSE on Natalie and Tobin talking intimately.

                    TOBIN
          I don't know what you see in me.
          I hope, I pray, it's not just -

                   NATALIE
          I'm wealthy too. We're more alike
          than you think, Melvy.

                    TOBIN
No, no, you would have avoided me. If
you knew me... back then.

                   NATALIE
Do you think I was popular?

                    TOBIN
I wasn't remotely liked. I was fat. A
nerd. Kids, they called me Tubby.

He attempts to brush it off and reclaim his
present status. Natalie is moved by his pain. She
lifts her glass.

                   NATALIE
And now you're a geek-turned-chic.
Lets toast to sweet revenge.

                    TOBIN
But I don't want revenge. The world,
it's so full of hate. I feel a need
to make a difference. Change things.
When you're the wealthiest man, you -
God, listen to me.
          (sighs)
I sound bitter, don't I?

                   NATALIE
I like it when you're bitter-sweet.

She CLINKS her glass to his and gets Tobin to
smile.

HART is watching her, then looks up at the
stars.

EXT. GRASSY KNOLL, 3RD FAIRWAY - DAY 2 - LATE
NIGHT

The group staggers to the top of a steep grassy
slope.

                    SAVAGE
You got us here, barely. Now what?

                    HART
Take a load off.

                    FIELD
          (collapses)
With pleasure.

                    HART
Lie on your backs. Vertical to the
slope. And simply relax.

Hart and Mia demonstrate this supine angle and
position.

                    MIA
Space yourselves apart. Stay still.

                    FIELD
          (slurs)
Easy for you to say.

                    SAVAGE
Is this the big payoff. Nirvana?

                    HART
Maybe a taste.

                    HILLER
Don't be stingy. A whole glass.

                    FIELD
          (laughs)
My head is already spinning.

                    HART
Close your eyes. Be silent.

TALKING and MUTTERING persist.

                    DOROTHY
    Shoosh!

SILENCE settles in. A gentle BREEZE is heard.

                    HART
    Open your eyes. What do you see?

DISSOLVE TO: A NIGHT SKY

                    SUZZIE (V.O.)
    A moon.

                    MICHELE (V.O.)
            (hiccups)
    Two moons.

                    DOROTHY (V.O.)
    Twinkling stars.

                    HILLER (V.O.)
    That's the atmosphere.

                    ZIT (V.O.)
    Pinpricks.

                    HART (V.O.)
    Try to imagine if those points of
    light were all connected.

                    TOBIN (V.O.)
    Circuitry.

                    FIELD (V.O.)
    Chaos.

                    HART (V.O.)
    Like our minds -

DISSOLVE TO: A VAST SEA OF STARS SURROUNDING A
GALAXY

                    HART
A delicate balance of connectivity.
        (beat)
Feel the earth's centrifugal pull.
Feel the force of gravity.
        (beat)
On average, our planet orbits the Sun
at a speed of 67,000 mph. Our star
circles the galaxy at about 560,000
mph. Concurrently the Milky Way is
moving 80 miles per second toward
Andromeda, another galaxy.
        (beat)
We're riding on a whirling chunk of
rock-liquid-gas hurtling at crazy
speeds end over end through space.
And we can't sense it or even know
it's happening. Except in concept.

Hiller is heard SNORING.

                    SUZZIE (V.O.)
A shooting star.

                    MICHELE (V.O.)
Pretty.

                    HART (V.O.)
We're all connected to one another in
more ways than we can imagine.

                    SUZZIE (V.O.)
How do you mean?

                    HART (V.O.)
By influences we can't perceive.

                    SAVAGE (V.O.)
        (scoffs)
He means God.

                    HART (V.O.)
I'm not talking about religion.

> DOROTHY (V.O.)
But God does exist.

> HART (V.O.)
God is our perception of reality.

> SAVAGE (V.O.)
Ironic. Coming from a fraud.

> HART (V.O.)
Everyone of us here is a fraud.

> DOROTHY (V.O.)
I'm not a fraud.

> HART (V.O.)
You may be the exception, Dorothy.

DISSOLVE TO: AN EXPANDING UNIVERSE WITH ENDLESS STARS.

> HART (V.O.)
Frauds. Because of self deception.
The universe has fooled us into
believing we perceive one reality.
Our sun delights and blinds us daily
with this notion. And yet a fraction
of what we sense is real.

> TOBIN (V.O.)
We're the ultimate paradox.

> DOROTHY (V.O.)
Then how do we know what's real?

CLOSE on Hart's quixotic smile.

> HART
We don't. Many realities coexist.

Hart rises, goes over to Hiller still SNORING.
He removes Hiller's glasses, quickly turns his
body with a push.

Hiller wakes, STARTLED, rolling down the grassy slope.

> HART
> But this is ours. So enjoy it. And
> sometimes we need a kick-start.

Hart nods at Mia who turns and rolls down the
slope too.

> HART
> Bad karma is like a bad habit, hard
> to break, to accept, and release.
> Time for some fun. Let go. Release.

There is a moment of paralysis. The attendees
question why they are on the slope of a golf
course at night in sheets.

A palpable uncertainty lingers, possible revolt
in the air, until Natalie initiates the next
move and shouts -

> NATALIE
> My turn!

She rolls down the slope LAUGHING like a wild
schoolgirl. Suzzie and Michele look at each
other, LAUGH and roll too. Sporadic SHOUTS from
the rest who follow. Except Savage.

> SAVAGE
> (stands)
> I'll see you at the bottom.

> HART
> A word of advice.

> SAVAGE
> Spare me.

> HART
> Bet on something that truly matters
> to you. That path leads to nirvana.

                    SAVAGE
     Fuck off.

Savage trudges drunkenly down the slope on foot.

Natalie rolls and bumps into Mia. Mia doesn't
reciprocate Natalie's smile. She gives back a
flicker of resentment.

                    NATALIE
     You're in love with Hart.

They both turn away and look back at -

Hart on the ridge. He waves, then SHOUTS,
launching his body down the slope. Tumbling past
Savage, he stops near Hiller.

Hart walks over and hands Hiller his glasses.

                    HART
     I believe these are yours.

                    HILLER
     Thank you. I thought I'd lost them.
     Wait. It was you who pushed me!

                    HART
     Guilty. I surprised you. Have fun?

                    HILLER
     I could've easily broken my neck.

                    HART
     Not likely. I know this hill well.
     The ground is soft and forgiving.

                    HILLER
     Well, I'm not.

Hiller grabs his wife's arm, pulling her along.

DOROTHY
Harold, it was fun. Admit it.

EXT. SAND TRAP - DAY 2 - MIDNIGHT

Tobin, having rolled into a bunker, lies gazing at stars.

EXT. ROW OF TENTS - LATER

Hiller holds the tent's flap open for his wife to enter.

DOROTHY
You look like a bedouin sheik.

HILLER
(gruff)
I am.

DOROTHY
Powerful. Sexy.

HILLER
(aroused)
Humm.

INT. TENT - LATER

Suzzie and Michele lie next to one another in sleeping bags.

SUZZIE
I can never see myself as pretty.

MICHELE
You must. These surgeons, they're like miracle workers.

SUZZIE
Thank you for coming with me.

                    MICHELE
          You need looking after.

Suzzie leans in, kisses Michele on the lips,
withdraws.

Taken aback, Michele turns over in her bag to
face away.

                    MICHELE
          Good night.

EXT. SPA BY SWIMMING POOL - LATER

The members of PISS sit in a bubbling spa
HUMMING.

INT. HART'S STUDY, Z-BLISS ESTATE - LATE NIGHT

DARKNESS. A PEN LIGHT REVEALS A FILE CABINET

Savage picks the lock. He rummages in the drawer. He pulls out a file and is shocked to see -

NAME ON FILE: "WILL SAVAGE (AKA MELIOR)"

                    SAVAGE
          You bastard.

EXT. VERANDA, Z-BLISS ESTATE - LATE NIGHT

Mia and Natalie sit in lounge chairs by the pool.

                    NATALIE
          Are we allowed to fraternize?

                    MIA
                 (direct)
          Why are you here?

                    NATALIE
          To be enlightened.

Natalie runs fingers through her hair and yawns.

                    NATALIE
          I didn't want to disappoint Melvin.

                    MIA
          But you don't love him.

                    NATALIE
          Is love so important?

                    MIA
          For some people.

                    NATALIE
          Said from one who is in love.

                    MIA
          We have a business arrangement. Which
          is none of your business.

                    NATALIE
          My mistake. Then you won't mind if I
          find myself attracted to him too?

                    MIA
          Don't mess things up.

A LOUD CLATTER startles Mia and Natalie. Russ
Field has collided with pool chairs and has
fallen.

                    FIELD
          Thank God. It's only you.

                    MIA
          Who did you think we were?

                    FIELD
          I thought... I... forget it.

Untangling himself from the chairs, he staggers
off.

INT. HART'S STUDY - LATE NIGHT

Savage is reading through the many files he's
discovered.

                    HART (O.C.)
        Find what you were looking for, Mr.
        Savage. Or do you prefer, Melior?

Savage looks up, caught. Hart stands at the
door. Savage, emboldened by his find, changes
from prey to predator.

                    SAVAGE
        A guru who spies on his patrons.

                    HART
        I like to be thorough.

                    SAVAGE
        Financial reports, psychological pro-
        files, detailed histories.

                    HART
        These are the tools necessary to
        provide you with what I promised.

                    SAVAGE
        Nirvana. Right.

Savage FLICKS on a lamp, aiming the beam of
light on Hart.

                    SAVAGE (O.C.)
        You're pretty cool for someone about
        to be exposed as a crook.

Hart flicks on the overhead light.

                    HART
        I have nothing to hide from you.

Hart approaches his desk. Savage backs away.

                    HART
You possess the heart of a gambler.

                    SAVAGE
Your point?

Savage has taken a letter opener off the desk.
Hart calmly rummages through a drawer and
removes a deck of cards.

                    HART
What did you wager with the devil?

                    SAVAGE
Go to hell.

                    HART
Fame? Fortune? A woman's love?

                    SAVAGE
Fuck off.

                    HART
I'm willing to bet my life. How much
are you willing to bet?

Savage wipes at perspiration on his forehead.

                    SAVAGE
The game's over, Hart. You lose.

                    HART
The game is never over.

                    SAVAGE
You're a fake, an admitted fraud.

                    HART
See, no tricks.

Hart spreads the cards face up. He scoops them
back, then shuffles and spreads the cards face
down on the desktop.

                    HART
    Pick one.

Savage glances at the door.

                    SAVAGE
    Are your gorillas outside? Waiting to
    stop me from leaving?

                    HART
    You can leave anytime, unharmed.

                    SAVAGE
    You're bluffing.

                    HART
    Call my bluff. Select a card.

                    SAVAGE
    Why should I?

                    HART
    Because I know you. You're going to
    pick the Queen of Hearts.

He places a hand to his heart, then leaves the
room.

                    HART (O.C.)
    She is the one you truly desire.

Savage cautiously moves to the door and peers
outside.

The cards, like a strong magnet, pull him back
toward them. He resists and climbs out a window
taking the letter opener.

Moments later he climbs back inside. He walks
back to the desk, hesitates, trying to decide.
He flips over a card.

CLOSE on the QUEEN OF HEARTS.

                    SAVAGE
          Son of a bitch!

He STABS the card with the letter opener. He
overturns another card, another. Every card is
the Queen of Hearts.

EXT. 3RD FAIRWAY, EARLY MORNING - DAY 3

The day portends to be another hot one. All
twelve of the participants, mostly hungover, sit
upon the grass.

There is a table with open coolers and bottles
of water.

Savage gives Hart a menacing look.

                    SUZZIE
          My bottom is getting wet.

                    MICHELE
          The grass is still dewy.

                    HART
          Be happy. You have reached Day 3. The
          home stretch to nirvana.

                    FIELD
          I'm dying for that tranquility.

                    HILLER
          I have a migraine.

                    HART
          From the tequila. The locus chant
          will blow away the psychic cobwebs
          stored deep in the third chakra.

Suzzie raises her hand.

                    SUZZIE
Isn't the third chakra about power
and ego control?

                    DOROTHY
We're only at the third chakra?

                    HART
Forget numbers.

                    SUZZIE
But nirvana is the seventh chakra.

                    HILLER
Seven! This is intolerable.

                    SAVAGE
Before we get to the sixth chakra, I
predict Hart goes down in flames.

Field, Hiller and Savage CHUCKLE.

                    DOROTHY
Stop that.

                    HART
It's okay. Laughter is cathartic.

Hart stands and signals for them to remain seated.

                    HART
Select a partner. Sit together with
your knees touching. Stare into each
other's face for half an hour. Do not
utter a word nor a sound. At the end
of that time, choose only one word to
describe your partner.

                    SUZZIE
One word?

                    HART
One word.

DOROTHY
I'm not sure I understand.

SAVAGE
As in fraud.

HART
Exactly. Or, for example, impotent.

Savage's face turns bright red.

SUZZIE
Okay, I get it.

HART
After that, pair up with another,
until you've experienced everyone.

HILLER
Jesus Christ.

TOBIN
That will take us six hours.

HART
There will be a lunch break.

Hart begins to walk toward the Z-Bliss estate.

HILLER
Wait just a god-damned minute!

Hart turns and smiles, placing his hands together.

HILLER
Where the hell are you going?

HART
To cool off in my pool. It's going to
be hot.

HILLER
I've had enough of your bullshit!

                    HART
Are you giving up? Surrendering?

                    HILLER
I'm a Marine. We never surrender.

                    HART
That's the spirit.

                    HILLER
You're one nasty son of a bitch!

                    HART
My mother was, at times, a bitch.
Manic-depressive. Yet, I loved her.

                    ZIT
I love me mum too.

Tobin turns to Natalie.

                    TOBIN
Are you regretting we came?

                    NATALIE
Don't be silly. It's exciting.

                    NED
Bloody fantastic, is it?

                    SUZZIE
Are you talking to me?

                    ZIT
This nirvana, you've had it?

                    MICHELE
First time for both of us.

                    HART
Be sure to keep hydrated. Drink lots
of water. Nirvana awaits.

                    FIELD
     Be a bull, Field. You're a bull.

Field, perspiring, glares back like a prize-
fighter, beaten and bleary eyed. He lifts the
water bottle to his face.

BOTTLE LABEL: "Z-BLISS FORTIFIED SPRING WATER."

                    HART
     You're all welcome to join me for
     cocktails at the pool. However, you
     would then forfeit your guarantee.
     And miss the bounties of nirvana.

Hart gives his trademark prayer salute, bids
them adieu.

                    SAVAGE
     Those details were never stated.

                    HART
     They were. It's in the fine print.

Hart strolls off WHISTLING.

Natalie lets go of Tobin's hand and stands.

                    NATALIE
     I think I'm going to join him.

                    TOBIN
     Natalie. But what about nirvana?

                    NATALIE
     I don't want it. Take mine.

                    TOBIN
     Natalie?

                    SAVAGE
     The numbers are uneven now, Z!

Hart's POV: He sees Natalie walking toward him.

                    HART
         Mia. Substitute for Natalie.

Mia glares at him, then transitions her face
into a smile.

                    MIA
         Who wants to be my partner?

Field raises his hand.

                    MIA
         Oh, goodie. Russ and I will now
         demonstrate the body position.

She sits and scoots her body into Field's, knees
touching. Her eyes drift toward Natalie walking
away with Hart.

                    FIELD
         You've had this nirvana before?

                    MIA
         Oh, I've experienced it many times.

                    FIELD
         Is it overrated?

                    MIA
         God, no. I take off all my clothes.

                    FIELD
              (speechless)

                    MIA
         But that's just me.

EXT. VERANDA - DAY 3

Natalie catches up to Hart. She walks beside him.

NATALIE
Your card said you were a grief
counselor. You were being naughty.

HART
As were you.

NATALIE
From a guru who fleeces his flock.

HART
Not an accurate job description.

NATALIE
Anarchist?

HART
I'm a pacifist.

NATALIE
Yet you flirt with disaster.

HART
I'm conducting an experiment.

They walk onto the veranda. Hart moves to the bar.

HART
I provide pleasure. What's yours?

NATALIE
Enlighten me.

Hart POPS a bottle of champagne, fills two
glasses, toasts.

HART
To nirvana.

NATALIE
Don't push your luck.
          (takes a sip)
There's mutiny in the air.

Hart considers this as they walk and sit by the
pool.

                    HART
          You don't care about nirvana?

                    NATALIE
          I like their music.

                    HART
          The soul is released from the body.
          No hatred or elusions. Said Buddha.

                    NATALIE
          You're not convincing me.

                    HART
          What will it take?

She sets her champagne glass on a table.

                    NATALIE
          Can you walk on water?

                    HART
          I haven't tried, yet.

                    NATALIE
          Are you that eager to drown?

Hart twirls his champagne.

                    HART
          What if I told you I was hoping to
          produce a miracle?

                    NATALIE
          I'd say you're in deep doo-doo.

She turns toward the attendees on the golf
course.

                    NATALIE
          And a hopeless romantic.

She unties the sash holding together her bedsheet.

                    NATALIE
          You do fascinate me though.

She stands, disrobes, and points her palms
together.

                    NATALIE
          I feel a need to cool off.

She dives naked into the pool.

Hart leans forward and watches as she swims
underwater.

CLOSE ON OF HER SHAPE-SHIFTING BODY MOVING ALONG
THE BOTTOM.

EXT. 3RD FAIRWAY, Z-BLISS ESTATE - DAY 3

Tobin and Dorothy are paired, staring at each other.

                    DEKE (O.C.)
          Time's up!

                    DOROTHY
          Sadness. Why are you so sad?

                    TOBIN
               (saddened)
          Not sure. You're... Angelic.

                    DEKE
          Keep your response to one word.

Field grins suggestively at Mia.

                    FIELD
          Ravishing.

                    MIA
    Rapacious.

Harold Hiller and Zit are paired, staring with
disdain.

                    HILLER
    Punk.

                    ZIT
    Fascist.

EXT. VERANDA - DAY 3

Hart, minus his robe, is in a swim suit. He's
distracted.

A SMALL MONITOR SHOWS MULTIPLE SCREEN VIEWS.

EXT. 3RD FAIRWAY - DAY 3

DEKE pretends to read a book. It's aimed at the
attendees.

EXT. VERANDA - DAY 3

Hart is sprinkled with water and looks up.

Natalie stands naked before him.

                    NATALIE
    What chakra am I at now?

She combs fingers through her hair and looks down.

CLOSE on Hart's monitor showing the workshop in
progress.

                    NATALIE
    Is there a method to your madness?

                    HART
    I believe there is.

                    NATALIE
     Impressive gobbledygook so far.

Hart sets his computer aside.

                    HART
     I've promised a moneyback guarantee -
     if I fail to deliver nirvana.

                    NATALIE
     And when you fail?

                    HART
     I won't.

                    NATALIE
     You're that sure of yourself?

                    HART
          (grins)
     We were fated to meet. That day I saw
     you seated in a lonely tower.

                    NATALIE
     It was on a park bench.

                    HART
     Like a princess in need of saving.

                    NATALIE
     Look who needs saving now.

                    HART
     You kissed me. Then ran away. Why?

                    NATALIE
     A kiss? I should stop doing that.

                    HART
     Do you kiss and run often?

She places the bedsheet poncho over her body.

                    NATALIE
        I'm a bad girl.

                    HART
        A court declared you innocent.

                    NATALIE
                 (darkening)
        So, you've been checking up on me.

                    HART
        I research all my attendees.

She lifts an eyebrow, assessing this new information.

                    NATALIE
        I'm not sure I approve.

                    HART
        Have lunch with me? My dining room,
        thirty minutes from now?

                    NATALIE
        Am I permitted to change?

Hart picks up his mobile devise, taps a message,
sends it.

                    HART
        Jake will meet you in the lobby with
        your luggage, then show you to a
        room. Unless you prefer a tent.

She smiles, says nothing, and saunters off.

EXT. HART'S BEDROOM - DAY 3

Mia enters unannounced. Hart is lying on the bed
reading Natalie's file. Mia sits beside him.

                    MIA
        How was your swim?

                    HART
I remained on dry land.

                    MIA
But she went in the pool. Naked?

                    HART
Swam underwater the whole length.

Mia pulls the file from his hands.

                    MIA
She's dangerous.

                    HART
I didn't invite her here, Mia.

                    MIA
You did. She's bad karma.

Hart considers this and looks into the skylight.

                    MIA
Assuming all screws and threads
haven't been stripped already, she is
bound to screw things up.

                    HART
My plan is foolproof.

                    MIA
Does the fool plan to share?

                    HART
She could be our wild card. This
could work to our advantage.

                    MIA
Whose advantage? How?
        (pouts)
Fine, tell me.

EXT. 3RD FAIRWAY - DAY 3

The attendees eat food pellets and drink bottled
water.

INT. DINING ROOM - DAY 3

Hart and Natalie and Mia sit before a luxurious
meal. Mia empties her wine glass. Hart, focused
on Natalie, asks -

> HART
> How's the moulard duck foie gras?

> MIA
> It's his favorite. Roast duck.

> HART
> Mia, you know I've many favorites.

> MIA
> He loves swordfish too. A masculine
> thing. The phallic aspect. I think
> you get the point. More wine?
> (reaches for it)
> I'll shut up. Imagine I'm not here.

> HART
> Mia.

> MIA
> Yes?

> HART
> I'd love more wine.

> NATALIE
> If you're pouring. Sure.

Mia stands, walks between them to pour. She
stops to stare at Natalie's low cut dress and
ample bosom.

                    MIA
It's a shame you had to keep those
under wrap all day.
          (laughs)
What I mean is I love your dress.

                  NATALIE
Thank you.

                    MIA
          (at the bottle)
Dead soldier. No one panic.

                   HART
I'll get another.

                    MIA
Sit! Let me.

Mia exits weaving, touching the door frame.

                   HART
Mia, she basically runs this place.

                  NATALIE
I can see that.

                  MIA (O.C.)
Thoughts! Hold them! I'd hate to miss
anything juicy!

Hart stares at Natalie. He is enthralled by her
beauty.

                   HART
I like you in that dress.

                  NATALIE
     Liar.

Mia returns with wine. She places the bottle
between her legs, inserts the corkscrew, twists
as she listens.

                    NATALIE
That tie-dyed robe's a monstrosity.

                      MIA
Whoa! Don't get any wild ideas.

They both look at Mia who pulls the cork out with a POP.

                      MIA
He's become celibate.

                    NATALIE
Oh?

                      MIA
I know! Shocker. When he told me.

                    NATALIE
Do tell.

Hart and Mia exchange looks as she pours wine in
his glass.

                     HART
Thanks.

                      MIA
My pleasure.

                    NATALIE
How long have you been celibate?

                     HART
       (evasive)
It's ... temporary.

                      MIA
Since he met this mystery woman. He
became inflamed with desire.

Hart narrows his eyes at Mia. She returns his
look.

                    HART
          Our guests?

                    MIA
          Right. Back to business.
                    (effusive)
          Nice to have met you Natalie. A shame
          you're out of the running. But
          engaged! Congrats. Be careful.

                    NATALIE
          Excuse me?

                    MIA
                    (at Hart)
          This one. He has a bad heart.

EXT. 3RD FAIRWAY - DAY 3

Deke holds out a tray of food to the attendees.

                    DEKE
          More sushi pellets?

                    SAVAGE
          I'd rather die.

Mia rejoins them wearing her bed sheet and a
silly grin.

                    MIA
          Hello! How was lunch? Whoooo!

Russ catches Mia as she trips. He helps her
back up.

                    MIA
          Rusty. So gallant. My hero.

                    FIELD
          Are you drunk?

She pinches thumb to finger. She CLAPS her hands.

                    MIA
     Resume positions. New partner.

EXT. VERANDA - DAY 3

Hart and Natalie sit on the patio, relaxing
after lunch. He indicates the cloudless blue
sky and points.

                    HART
     The stars are beautiful.

                    NATALIE
     If you insist.

                    HART
     Beautifully hidden. Always present.

                    NATALIE
     It must be difficult for you.

                    HART
     What?

                    NATALIE
     Being so optimistic.

                    HART
     Yes, a burden to be manically happy
     all the time. Wanting to see the best
     in everyone. It's pure hell.

                    NATALIE
     You're a man of smoke and mirrors.

                    HART
     Natalie, shame on you. I represent
     the essence of human existence.

                    NATALIE
          (seriously)
     What are you trying to accomplish?

                    HART
That's a good question.

                    NATALIE
I thought so.

BEEP-BEEP-BEEP. Hart shuts off his wristwatch
alarm.

                    HART
I need to attend to my flock. We
should do this again. Tonight?

Natalie lifts an eyebrow and stands.

                    NATALIE
I'll be changing in my room.
Try not to spook the herd.

EXT. 3RD FAIRWAY - DAY 3

Trancelike, the attendees sit cross-legged,
paired, staring into each another's eyes.

                    DEKE
     Time.

Mia wakes, having dozed off. Tobin looks into
her eyes.

                    MIA
     Oh... Hi.

                    TOBIN
Do you mean elevation? Stature?

                    MIA
No. Let me think. Compassionate.

Tobin is pleased. He says to her -

                    TOBIN
     Adorable.

MIA
I am?

TOBIN
He doesn't deserve you.

MIA
Who?

Hart appears upon the ridge, strolling toward the green.

SAVAGE
Well look who deigned to show up.

HART
Did everyone receive enlightenment?

Hart is accosted by dazed, confused, weary, hostile eyes.

HART
Good. That would be premature.

Natalie arrives. She sits beside Tobin. He looks at her. She looks at Mia, who looks at Tobin, who looks at Hart, who evades eye contact with all until Natalie settles in.

Hiller glares with intensity at Hart.

HILLER
When do I get my money back?

SAVAGE
Direct deposits or cash. No checks.

HART
Mia, if you'd be so kind to assist.

Mia stands and walks to the three arriving golf carts.

                    HILLER
          Finally. Are we playing golf?

                    HART
          Spiritual chanting and dancing.

                    ZIT
          Bloody hell.

Mia and the three bodyguards pass out musical
instruments - drums, cymbals, flutes, bells,
tambourines.

                    HART
          Only one chakra challenge remains.
          Go for the top chakra. Gold ring.

                    SUZZIE
          But it's so hot.

                    HART
          Keep hydrating.

                    DOROTHY
          I feel something already. I do.

                    SAVAGE
                (suspicious)
          Fortified? What'd you put in this?

BOTTLE LABEL: "Z-BLISS FORTIFIED SPRING WATER."

                    HART
          Spring water. Crystals. Antitoxins.
          All natural. The difference you feel
          is in your mind. Modified by the
          ambience and the meditations.

                    HILLER
          I'd rather slaughter you at golf.
          That would be my idea of nirvana.

Savage and Field CHUCKLE.

Hart leans down, plucks blades of grass, displays them.

                    HART
          The earth can be a bitter place. Not
          to everyone's liking. At times, hard
          to define. An acquired taste.

Hart places the grass in his mouth, chews, and swallows.

                    HART
          Forget who you think you are. Dismiss
          the illusion of self worth. Labels.
          Titles. Levels. Gender. Status.
          Release these manufactured notions of
          judgement from the mind. Search your
          soul. Nirvana awaits.

Mia hands Field a strand of bronze bells.

                    MIA
          I call this part a dionysian romp.

                    FIELD
          Will you be dancing naked?

                    MIA
          You never know.

                    HART
          Chant. Dance. Release. Enjoy.

Mia gives Hart a flicker of a smile before breaking into a nonsense CHANTING, dancing, BONGING on a goatskin drum. Dorothy SHAKES her tambourine, stands, grabs her husband.

                    DOROTHY
          Release yourself, Harold. Let go.

                         HILLER
                    (shakes her off)
          He's not getting me to hop around
          like a god-damned Energizer Bunny!

The group is far from unified. A few stand,
start to move.

Hart bids them adieu with his salute. Hiller gets
up fast.

                         HILLER
          Where are you off to now!

The movement and chanting stop. Hart turns and
bows.

                         HART
          To hit some balls. Tennis anyone?

                         NATALIE
          I'll play.

                         HART
          Wonderful.

Mia resumes BEATING her drum. Natalie whispers
to Tobin -

                         NATALIE
          I almost forgot. This is yours.

She slips the diamond engagement ring onto his
pinky finger.

                         TOBIN
          Natalie, what are you saying?

                         NATALIE
          You're way too good for me.

Mia POUNDS her drum louder. She WHOOPS and
CHANTS —

                    MIA
        Rum-a-dumb-dumb, Rum-a-dumb-dumb

Field is startled by the BEATING drums.

DISOLVE TO: INDIANS SURROUNDING FIELD IN A TRIBAL
GRAND JURY

                  FIELD (V.O.)
        What the hell.

                    HART
        Doubles, anyone? Last call.

                   SAVAGE
        I'll stand on my head and fart for an
        hour if that'll make you lose.

                    HART
        Farting is a lower chakra release.

Dorothy TOOTS a flute, hops past Hiller. He
swats at her.

                   HILLER
        Stop that, Dorothy.

Filled with bliss, Dorothy takes hold of Suzzie
who grabs Michele's hand. They SHRIEK and LAUGH
and start a daisy chain. They grab the members
of PISS, who reel in Tobin, who grabs Hiller,
who pushes away. He folds his arms.

                   HILLER
        I don't care who the hell you are.

Savage walks up to Hiller and BANGS a snakeskin
drum.

                   SAVAGE
        That fraud is going down-down-down.

Hiller RATTLES his beaded gourd ominously,
adding -

> HILLER
> As is dead—dead—dead!

Savage frowns and his conspiratorial grin fades.

EXT. TENNIS COURT - DAY 3

Hart hands Natalie a tennis racket but she
refuses it.

> NATALIE
> I don't really play.
> (at her sheet)
> Isn't this a dress code violation?

They walk to the ball server machine. Hart picks
up stray balls and drops them into the basket
holder.

> NATALIE
> How do you work this thing?

> HART
> Aim and shoot.

Hart leaps over the net. He positions himself to
receive.

A ball SOARS high over his head and STRIKES the
fence.

> HART
> At me.

EXT. TENNIS COURT - LATER

Natalie FIRES a ball. Hart KNOCKS it back.

> NATALIE
> Care to share your secret?

                    HART
          I may have enhanced the water.

                    NATALIE
          To achieve what?

                    HART
          Ecstacy. Or some facsimile.

Hart swings and HITS another ball over the net.

                    HART
          Imagine a world in black and white.
          Marvelous rich shadows. The dark, the
          light. The exquisite contrasts.

He WACKS back another ball.

                    HART
          And we accept this as reality.
          Then one day, quite by accident,
          color is discovered. How can one not
          inform the world that this new
          reality exists?

She gestures toward the beauty of their surroundings.

                    NATALIE
          I have breaking news for you.

                    HART
          It was a metaphor.

                    NATALIE
          Historically, the messengers of
          change are ridiculed. Put to death.

Hart dodges the next ball. He holds up a hand
for a break.

                    HART
          If I calculated correctly, one of
          three outcomes will occur soon.

                    NATALIE
    In your world of bliss?

                     HART
    Bliss is the absence of suffering.
    Achieving nirvana is a fallacy. To
    suffer. To be happy. Yin and Yang.

                    NATALIE
               (laughs)
    You're a hollow man in search of his
    insubstantial self.

                     HART
    Hey, stop seeing through me.

EXT. 3RD GREEN - DAY 3

Aerial view of retreat participants DANCING and
CHANTING around the flag pole. Their energy is
flagging.

EXT. 3RD GREEN - DAY 3 - MOMENTS LATER

Most of the group has collapsed on the grass.
They gulp bottled water, squirt it in their
mouths, on their heads.

Savage is scrutinizing the bottled water label
again.

Tobin is circling the green, exploring its edges
as if he has hit a firewall, searching for a way
beyond.

Field is cowering in a sand bunker and peers over
its edge.

DISOLVE TO: A MOB OF ANGRY PEOPLE GATHERING ON
THE VERANDA

                    FIELD
    I'm doomed. They've found me.

The CHANTS from PISS turn into ACAPPELLA. They sound good.

Suzzie and Michele gaze transfixed into each other faces.

> SUZZIE
> Look what we've become.

> MICHELE
> I don't feel real anymore.

> SUZZIE
> No, you're beautiful.

Suzzie strokes Michele's face, leans forward. They kiss.

Savage is disturbed by the display of lesbian love.

DISOLVE TO: TWO WOMEN IN BED MAKING LOVE

> WOMAN (O.C.)
> No one satisfies me like you do.
> (moans)
> You're more man than he'll ever be.

Savage hears LAUGHTER. He stands, walks off in a daze, falls off the green into a sand trap. Onto Field who SCREAMS.

Dorothy emits a CHIRP. She rises, flaps her arms as if they were wings, and runs down the slope after a swan.

> DOROTHY
> Too-wee-too-wee-too-wee-too-wee!

Hiller stares stupefied at his wife flying away.

> HILLER
> (at Mia)
> Am I the only sane one here?

Angered, Hiller storms over to Deke reading on a golf cart.

                    HILLER
     I need to use the head! Get off.

Hiller grabs Deke who SHRIEKS as he's tossed to the ground.

Suzzie and Michele point at Hiller departing in the cart.

                    SUZZIE
     He can't do that. Can he?

                    MIA
     I'd say he just did.

                    MICHELE
     I need to pee badly too.

Mia points to a grove of trees.

EXT. TENNIS COURT - DAY 3

Hart, in his swimsuit, crouches at the net.

                    NATALIE
     I've made you sweat.

She FIRES another ball. Hart dashes and SWATS it back.

INSERT - COMPUTER ON BENCH VIBRATING, RED LIGHT FLASHING.

EXT. STORAGE AREA ENTRANCE - DAY 3

Hiller stops the cart, gets out holding a golf towel. He grips both ends. JAKE blocks his way, fists on his hips.

                    HILLER
        I want my luggage. I'm leaving.

                    JAKE
        You need permission before —

Hiller SWATS Jake in the crouch with a SNAP of
the towel.

                    JAKE
        Ouch! Hey! Stop that!

                    HILLER
        Give me the god-damned keys!

He SWAT-SNAPS again. Jake trips on a curb, falls
backwards. His robe parts to reveal he's wearing
women's lace panties.

                    HILLER
        The keys, girly boy! Now.

Jake unclips the keys from his sash, hands them
to Hiller.

EXT. TENNIS COURT - DAY 3

Hart is collecting balls around the court with Natalie.

INT. STORAGE AREA - DAY 3

Hiller finds his luggage, opens the duffle bag,
removes the gun. He crosses himself with the
weapon, then leaves.

EXT. TENNIS COURT - DAY 3

Natalie trails her finger down Hart's sweaty chest.

EXT. 3RD GREEN - DAY 3

OVERVIEW of Hiller in the cart, ROARING past the
others.

CLOSE on Hiller holding the gun as he steers.

CUT TO: Mia running fast to catch up, attendees in tow.

EXT. TENNIS COURT - DAY 3

Hart stands at the net as Natalie feeds the ball machine.

                    HART
          What made you call off the wedding?

                    NATALIE
          You should know my husband dropped
          dead on his own. Wasn't my doing.
                    (fires a ball)
          I'm not that bad a person.

                    HART
          Not a hideous spider?

                    NATALIE
          Calculating. That's all.

                    HART
          Should I be worried?

                    NATALIE
          The sex? You like taking risks.

He smiles, SWATS a new ball over the net.

                    HART
          I'd gladly risk dying for you.

Natalie frowns, sees Hiller approaching with a gun.

                    NATALIE
          How about him?

EXT. PATHWAY TO TENNIS COURT - DAY 3

Hiller has a crazed expression of determination.
He kicks open the metal gate. The gun is aimed
at Hart.

                    HILLER
          This is for the money you conned out
          of me! And all the others!

Natalie retreats from Hart who backs against the
fence.

                    HILLER
          And for my son! He hated frauds!

Mia POUNCES on Hiller from behind, clawing and
knocking off his glasses. Hiller flings her off
- CRASHING her into the fence. Hiller, without
his glasses, starts FIRING.

Suzzie and Michele SCREAM.

Bullets STRIKE the net, fence, clay surface,
missing Hart.

                    HILLER
          Did I get that bastard?

Savage enters the court and wrestles the gun
from Hiller.

                    SAVAGE
          You're blind. Let me shoot that fuck.
          It all makes sense now. We achieve
          nirvana by shooting you.
          How many points for a leg? An arm?
               (distracted)
          What the -

Natalie is naked, dancing between the shooter
and target - waving the bedsheet in the air like
a performing gymnast.

                    HILLER
     Shoot him!

Hart spreads his arms and declares -

                    HART
     Look! Natalie has reached nirvana!

                    SAVAGE
     Bullshit! She's naked. That's all.

Hiller blindly searches to find his glasses.

                    FIELD
     And what a vision she is!

                    SUZZIE
     I want nirvana! That's not fair.

                    MICHELE
     Wasn't she disqualified?

Suzzie pulls her bedsheet off and mimics
Natalie's dance.

Savage aims the gun at Hart but can't pull the
trigger.

                    SAVAGE
     Oh, fuck this! Fuck it all!

With imploding disgust he turns the gun on himself, points the gun to his head and pulls the
trigger. CLICK.

                    SAVAGE
     My luck! No more bullets left.

Savage opens the chamber. Sees bullets. Shocked
the gun hadn't fired, he walks off, tossing it
outside the gate.

Dorothy appears on a grassy knoll flapping her arms.

Tobin finds Hiller's glasses, walks over, taps his arm.

Hiller spins around, blindly squinting.

>   TOBIN
>   You almost killed a man. What the
>   hell is the matter with you?

Hiller grasps for his glasses but misses.

>   HILLER
>   I'm the sane one here.

>   TOBIN
>   A jury might conclude otherwise.

Hiller snatches his glasses back, places them on his head.

>   HILLER
>   That man deserves to be shot.

Hiller forms a gun with his hand, cocks, fires at Hart.

>   TOBIN
>   Care for your wife. She's an angel.
>   (at Dorothy)
>   As lovely as my Natalie.

Hiller sees Natalie stark naked. His wife is outside the fence dancing and flapping her arms. Hiller SLUGS Tobin.

>   HILLER
>   Software. Meet Hardware.

Tobin DROPS to the clay surface. He loses consciousness.

INSERT: A SPECTACULAR LIGHT SHOW OF INTERACTING STARS.

PISS, on the fairway, HARMONIZE like a Greek chorus.

Dorothy TWEETS and flies past them waving.

Suzzie is SCREAMING, demanding nirvana. Michele SLAPS her hard. Suzzie cradles her face like it is fragile art.

> SUZZIE
> That was mean.

> MICHELE
> Yes, it was. You needed grounding.

They hug. Mia walks past them up to a shaken Hart.

> MIA
> I warned you.

Natalie twirls as she dances past them.

> MIA
> You can cut the nirvana act.

CUT TO: Hiller finding his gun in the grass by the gate.

> DOROTHY (V.O.)
> Look, Harold! I'm free. A bird.

Hiller GRUMBLES, ignoring her as she flutters around him.

Tobin has a exuberant grin as he approaches Hart.

> TOBIN
> It happened! The stars connected!

> HART
> (feigns understanding)
> Congratulations.

                    TOBIN
      I should have never doubted you.

CUT TO: Mia's incredulous expression.

Field overhears. He is edgy, paranoid, and
approaches them.

                    FIELD
      Well, none of it worked for me.

Hiller storms into the tennis court, aims the
gun at Hart but lacks his prior conviction.
Field raises his hands.

                    FIELD
      I give up! I surrender! Don't -

                    HILLER
      I'm not the police, you idiot.

With downcast eyes, Field walks toward Hiller,
then dodges past him and runs out the tennis
court gate.

CLOSE on MIA at the ball machine. She aims and
shoots.

A ball HITS Hiller's head and his glasses fly
off.

Mia lowers the machine and FIRES again.

Hiller's crotch receives a direct HIT. He DROPS
the gun.

Natalie picks it up and walks out of the tennis
court.

                              DISSOLVE TO:

EXT. 1ST FAIRWAY - DAY 3

Hart is walking beside Mia amidst a lingering
COMMOTION.

Dorothy circles and stops next to her husband who
is beside himself, compulsively repenting and
shaking his head.

              HILLER
    Jesus, I almost killed a man. What
    came over me? I'm not a murderer.

              DOROTHY
    I know, Dear. And I'm not a bird.

              HILLER
    That's a relief.

PISS, off in the distance, HARMONIZE to another
song.

Savage sits at the edge of a fairway with his
head in hands.

Field is hiding behind the trunk of an oak tree.

Trailing behind Hart like shell-shocked sheep are
Suzzie, Michele, and Tobin. Natalie joins them.
Her bedsheet is on.

Hart stops, turns, and says in a loud voice -

              HART
    Cocktails are at six-thirty. A five-
    star dinner follows at seven.
    Questions and grievances will be
    addressed at that time.

As Hart walks off, Mia approaches Natalie.

              MIA
    I give up. Where is it?

                    NATALIE
        Where is what?

                      MIA
        The gun.

                    NATALIE
        I tossed it over there.

She points to a water hazard near the tennis court.

                      MIA
        Your distraction helped. Thanks.

                    NATALIE
        You were the one who saved him.

                      MIA
        I wanted you gone. Now I'm glad you
        stayed.

Mia runs and catches up to Hart.

                      MIA
        Are you happy now?

                     HART
        Ecstatic.

                      MIA
        You realize you almost died.

Hart gives her a nonchalant shrug.

Mia wants to be mad at him but falters into a smile.

                     HART
        Natalie was sure something. She saved
        the day, don't you think?

                      MIA
            (stung)
        Yes. She is definitely something.

Mia walks faster, moving ahead, suddenly running away.

                    HART
          Mia. What is it? What's wrong?

EXT. HILLER'S TENT - DUSK

Dorothy is CRYING on her sleeping bag. Her head
is covered by her bedsheet. Hiller sits beside
her, rubbing her arm.

                    DOROTHY
          I embarrass you. An embarrassment is
          what I am. I don't mean to be.
              (cries)
          I miss our Howie too, you know.

He removes the sheet off her face, leans down,
kisses her.

                    HILLER
          Dorothy, I know that. I... was too
          consumed by my own grief... I -
              (grimaces)
          Why did he do it? Why? Write those
          words: "I can no longer accept the
          hypocrisy of the world anymore."

                    DOROTHY
          He was too smart. Too sensitive.

                    HILLER
          What did he mean? Did he mean me? Did
          I push him too hard?

                    DOROTHY
          You loved him. Howie knew that.

                    HILLER
          Hillers are made of stronger stuff.
          That's what my father beat into me.
              (swipes at tears)
          Damn it. I hate this.

> DOROTHY
> It's okay to cry. We knew Howie was
> different. He'd want us to be happy.

Hiller's body suddenly heaves into uncontrollable
SOBBING.

> DOROTHY
> Oh, Harold. What is to become of us?

EXT. GOLF COURSE - DUSK

Savage is seated on an oak tree branch and muttering -

> SAVAGE
> emilyemilyemilyemilyemilyemily

EXT. VERANDA AND POOL - DUSK

The foursome, PISS, relax in a bubbling spa,
SINGING opera.

EXT. GOLF COURSE - DUSK

Tobin is on his back in a bunker. A sand castle
beside him. He gazes at the diamond ring on his
pinky as stars appear.

EXT. VERANDA - DUSK

Suzzie and Michele rock together in a hammock.

> SUZZIE
> We are pretty, aren't we?

> MICHELE
> But ugly on the inside. Maybe you
> were right. We should give away our
> money to charities. All of it.

Suzzie pulls away and SLAPS Michele's cheek.

                    SUZZIE
Now you're being pretty. Stupid.

EXT. TOPIARY GARDEN - DUSK

Russ Field comes upon an intriguing garden.
He enters. It has tall hedges like walls and
multiple circular paths.

OVERVIEW of LABYRINTH and Field becoming lost in
its maze.

INT. MIA'S BEDROOM, Z-BLISS - NIGHT

Mia is CRYING into a pillow on her bed. There is
a KNOCK.

                    MIA
        What?

                    HART
        May I enter?

                    MIA
        Wait.

Mia wipes her eyes, straightens the bed, grabs a
book.

                    MIA
        Okay.

Hart enters wearing matching white silk pants
and shirt.

Mia, in panties and bra, hair mussed, looks over
her book.

                    HART
        Why aren't you dressed?

                    MIA
        What's wrong with this?

                    HART
     Nothing. I find it rather -

                    MIA
     Don't.

She sets the book upon her chest, looks directly
at him.

Hart lingers, moves across the room, peers out
the window.

                    HART
     Thank you for saving my life.

                    MIA
     Don't mention it.

                    HART
     You know how much you mean to me.

                    MIA
     Actually, I don't. Go on.

                    HART
     This is awkward. I never thought I.
     What I mean is... I...

Hart shakes his head, searching for words. Mia
sits up.

                    MIA
     Go on. I'm interested.

                    HART
     Mia, you're really the only person
     I've ever trusted. I rely on you.

                    MIA
     This is about her.

                    HART
     You don't like Natalie, do you?

                    MIA
        She's very charming.

Hart brightens. He rubs his palms together.

                    HART
        I feel like - like we are alike.

                    MIA
        You definitely are.

                    HART
        What should I do?

Mia slides off the bed, stands and walks over to
a closet.

                    MIA
        You should marry her. Fuck your soul
        mate. Die in her arms.

She holds up a dress.

                    MIA
        Will this do?

                    HART
        You're jealous.

                    MIA
        No.

She steps into the dress, white, strapless,
pulls it up.

                    HART
        You are.

                    MIA
        Stop it. Help me with this.

He steps over, zips her up, fastens the top of
her dress.

                    HART
     I'm a fraud. We both know that.   But
     I'd never ever deceive you.

Mia turns around and stares at him for an
eternal second.

                    MIA
     You take people's money, Zack. And
     give them nothing. Except a grasp at
     hope. And some worthless bliss.

She rummages through a jewelry box.

                    MIA
     And yet they keep coming back. Even
     though you give them nothing. Admit
     it. Because you're the best. A fraud,
     yes. A very good one.

She holds up a necklace and turns for him to
clasp it on.

                    MIA
     I'm not angry because you think
     you're in love. I'm angry because
     you're willing to... Forget it.

                    HART
     I thought we had an understanding.

She snaps on a matching bracelet.

                    MIA
     We do. I understand.

                    HART
     We're still good then? You're sure?

                    MIA
     For later, you mean. I'm good.

                      121

                    HART
        You really are my best friend.

                    MIA
        I really need to pee, if that's all
        you came to tell me.

She walks into the bathroom, closes the door.

                    MIA
        Because of you, wonderful things do
        happen. I don't know how. They do.

SILENCE follows. Unsure what to say, Hart
quietly leaves.

INT. MIA'S BATHROOM - NIGHT

She sits on the toilet seat in her dress, hands
on face.

                    MIA
        You enlightened me. Which is why I
        stayed with you.

She FLUSHES. She washes her hands, then rubs
away tears.

                    MIA
        And the reason I'm still here.

Opening the door, she is surprised to find the
room empty.

INT. NATALIE'S BEDROOM - NIGHT

Natalie is dressed to kill in a black and gold
lace dress. At the mirror she blows at her
fingernails, drying polish.

There is a three-tap KNOCKING.

                    NATALIE
    Who is it?

She opens the door. Hart holds a champagne
bottle and two stemmed glasses. Also a rose. He
hands her the rose.

                    HART
    Your knight in shining silk.

Natalie smiles, acts blasé. She gestures for him
to enter.

                    NATALIE
    I approve.

                    HART
    You look divine.

He goes to a bar, uncorks the bottle, fills two
glasses.

He hands her a glass and CLINKS his glass to hers.

As he reaches for her hand holding the rose, she
says -

                    NATALIE
    Thorns. Wet nails. Caution.

                    HART
        (humored)
    We're alike, I believe. In mind, but
    not in body. Thank God. And bound
    together like rose petals.

                    NATALIE
    We're a flower? Not very original.

                    HART
    Most flowers make me sneeze.

She sips her champagne, her lips moist, renewed smile.

> NATALIE
> You're okay at this. I predict, you
> and I, we will be a perfect fit.

> HART
> Perfection. I wonder if it exists.

> NATALIE
> Is that my cue to disrobe?

> HART
> I've already seen you naked.

> NATALIE
> I hope you approve.

> HART
> Absolutely. You saved my life.

> NATALIE
> Now you're deeply indebted. You owe
> me no less than total satisfaction.

She sets down the rose, her glass. She reaches
back, UNZIPS her dress. It falls. She's naked,
except for red panties.

> HART
> Are those... leather?

> NATALIE
> Licorice. Edible. Come. Eat me.

Hart becomes distracted by handcuffs on the dresser.

> NATALIE
> Do you need a starting pistol? Or,
> maybe I should take out my whip.

Her coy smile beguiles. She lies waiting upon the bed.

A DISTANT SCREAM is heard from somewhere outside.

Hart responds, moves to the sliding door, onto the balcony.

EXT. BALCONY, Z-BLISS - NIGHT

In the distance, Hart sees a whiteness fluttering upon the golf course like the sail of a ship. It's Mia in her white dress feeding swans by a water hazard under a full moon.

EXT. 1ST FAIRWAY - NIGHT

Mia notices Hart standing on the balcony. Then Natalie, who appears naked. Her arms embrace him, pulling him inside.

Mia's fingers are nipped by an impatient swan.

> MIA
> (scolding)
> Behave, or you'll get nothing.

EXT. LABYRINTH, CENTER OF MAZE - NIGHT

A disheveled Field approaches a figure in the moon-light. It's a large sculpture. It's a replica of the charging bull on Wall Street. But decapitated. Its severed head and horns touch the ground. The neck, minus head, forms a plaque:

PLAQUE: "GOD CANNOT BE MOCKED. A MAN REAPS WHAT HE SOWS."

INT. NATALIE'S ROOM - NIGHT

Natalie reels Hart back inside, her body presses into his.

> NATALIE
> Back to coupling.

Hart appears dazed, changed, as if only half there.

                    NATALIE
We'll make a formidable force.

                    HART
About that. About who I am.

                    NATALIE
               (teases)
I already know who you are.

                    HART
You don't.

Realizing something is amiss, she lets go of him.

                    NATALIE
I forgot. You're celibate.

                    HART
     I'm not.

                    NATALIE
Good. Because I want you. Bad.

                    HART
Problem is, I love someone else.

Natalie picks up her glass and downs the champagne.

                    NATALIE
Very low marks for your timing.
               (darkening)
Let's try another approach.

She opens her luggage, removes a leather riding
crop. With it she SLAPS the bed. Hart flinches.

                    HART
What the hell's that for?

                    NATALIE
Show me the depths of your sorrow.

> HART
> Excuse me?

> NATALIE
> You need to do better than that.

She WHIPS the side of his silk pants.

> HART
> Jesus! I'm sorry I upset you. Okay?

> NATALIE
> Not okay.

She SWIPES at his crotch. He jumps back to avoid it.

> HART
> It became clear only moments ago —

She brandishes the whip and SNAPS it.

> HART
> How much I love her.

> NATALIE
> That's sweet. Mia?

She SWATS his shoulder. He hops onto the bed.
He hops off to the other side. She moves around,
has him cornered.

> HART
> Natalie, I swear, I fully intended to
> have sex with you. It's just -

> NATALIE
> I broke off my engagement. To a
> multi-billionaire! To bet on you -
> this dark horse.
> (swats him)
> Now you owe me. Perform.

Hart LEAPS onto the bed to avoid the whip.

                    HART
I'm a cad, all right?

                    NATALIE
          (points)
Get down. On all fours.

                    HART
Natalie, you picked the wrong horse.
It happens.

Natalie SNAPS her whip and Hart BOLTS for the door.

INT. BALLROOM - NIGHT

The attendees are regrouped, redressed,
refreshed. With drinks in hands, eating an
assortment of delectables - crab cakes, caviar -
they stand around waiting for the host.

Field enters wearing a tuxedo. His face has
scratch marks.

The Hillers hold martinis. Dorothy's arm is
hooked to his. Savage, sipping a glass of
Scotch, walks over to Hiller.

                    SAVAGE
I bet this prick doesn't even show.

                    HILLER
Does it really matter?

Savage is perplexed by Hiller's complaisant
demeanor and drifts off to refresh his drink.

Natalie enters the room as Mia is exiting. They
both stop. Natalie is condescending for all to
see and hear.

                    NATALIE
You'll be pleased to know your boss
has forsaken his vow of celibacy.

> NATALIE (cont.)
> You can congratulate us. I must have
> done something right, because he
> proposed to me. And I accepted.

Mia tries but fails to appear unfazed by this news.

> MIA
> Well, congratulations.

> NATALIE
> Thank you. You might consider search-
> ing employment elsewhere.

Natalie lights a cigarette. She inhales, blows
out smoke.

> NATALIE
> Although, you'd be a help to have
> around to arrange our wedding.

Natalie turns and leaves to mingle with the others.

Mia stands there, stunned. She sees Hart turning
a corner. He smiles and stops to whisper something. She pushes past him.

> MIA
> Don't say anything.

> HART
> Mia?

> MIA
> Not now!

She storms down the hallway.

> HART
> Mia, wait! I need to —

Stopping in the foyer, she turns and SHOUTS -

                    MIA
Everyone is waiting for you!
          (in tears)
Except for me! I'll be gone!

                    HART
Mia, what happened?

                    MIA
Go to hell! I hate you!

She runs up the stairs. Hart hesitates, not sure
which way to go, turns to face a silenced room.
He braves a smile.

                    SAVAGE
Trouble in paradise?

Natalie starts to CLAP. A spatter of applause
follows.

                    HART
Good evening. I hope.

INT. MIA'S BEDROOM - NIGHT

Mia opens a suitcase on her bed. A gun is inside.

INT. BALLROOM - NIGHT

Hart nods at Deke standing by the kitchen door.
He exits.

Field nervously twitches as he sees the body-
guard leave.

                    HART
Are there any questions?

                    SAVAGE
When do we get our money back?

                    HART
Ah, but I saw you seated in a tree.
Enthralled. Did you find nirvana?

Savage blinks, embarrassed, defiant.

                    SAVAGE
No. I like trees. So what?

                    HART
Cash? Or a direct deposit?

                    SAVAGE
First, I want a show of hands. Who,
if anyone, achieved nirvana?

The attendees look around. Tobin raises a hand.
Then Suzzie and Michele. The members of PISS give
a unified fist salute. Dorothy lifts her hand and
pulls at her husband's hand.

                    HILLER
              (whispers)
Dorothy, let go. Not here.

                    SAVAGE
You can't all be serious.

                    FIELD
I'll take that, uh, refund.

                    SAVAGE
There. Two dissatisfied customers.
          (at Natalie)
And what about you?

                    NATALIE
Oh, I intend to have him pay me.

                    MICHELE
You were disqualified!

Hart gestures for them to turn around.

                    131

                    HART
          I am a man of my word.

Deke, Jake, and Jess wheel in a table holding
twelve stacked briefcases. Deke opens one,
displaying bundles of money.

                    HART
          I will be returning your money, to
          anyone who feels dissatisfied with
          the results.

Blindsided by this, Savage furrows his brow.

                    SAVAGE
          The money is probably fake.

                    HART
          You're all welcome to inspect it.
          But first, I would like to say a few
          words about love -

A unified GASP comes from the attendees as they
back away.

                    MIA (O.C.)
          He knows nothing about love!

Hart turns.

Mia stands in the doorway. Her hands are trem-
bling, holding a gun pointed at Hart.

                    HART
          Mia.

                    MIA
          I'd advise you all take your money
          now and run as fast as you can -
          because this man will screw you any-
          way he possibly can.

                    HART
         That's not true.

Hart moves toward her.

                    MIA
         Don't!

Hart stops.

                    MIA
         I know this because I've learned
         everything about lying and cheating
         and betrayal - from him!

Her hands shake. A finger is crooked on the trigger.

                    HART
         Mia, talk to me. What's wrong?

                    MIA
         Wrong!? Tell them! Tell them all how
         you plan to cheat them. Tell -

The gun FIRES, surprising Mia.

Hart staggers back. Bloods seeps through his
fingers onto his silk shirt spreading from an
entry point near his heart.

                    HART
         Mia. I wanted... I love you.

Hart collapses to the floor.

Mia drops the gun. She moves toward him. Deke
restrains her. Jake and Jess rush over to help
Hart.

                    DEKE
         Call 9-1-1!

The attendees reach for cell phones they don't have.

DEKE
Jake! Jess! Do it now! Quick!

OVERVIEW of Mia. She is CRYING and clinging to
Deke.

HART (V.O.)
It's been said that as you die you
float out of your physical body and
look down on the shell of yourself.

OVERVIEW of Jake frantically dialing on his
mobile phone while Jess' hands attempt to stop
the bleeding.

MIA (O.C.)
He said he loved me.

HART (V.O.)
As your life bursts into that final
detonation, sucked into a swirling
tunnel of light, and loved ones
appear to you in a veil of mist...
(sighs)
That never happened.

SMASH CUT TO:

The attendees converge around Hart but keep their
distance.

Savage lights a cigarette to calm himself and
mutters -

SAVAGE
Breaking News: Fraud Dead At Bliss.

Field goes to inspect the money but is stopped,
HEARING -

JAKE
Hey! A man's been shot! Back off!

                    FIELD
              (raises hands)
        My bad. Bad form. You're right.

EXT. DRIVEWAY - NIGHT

Police cars and ambulances arrive with WAILING
sirens.

INT. BALLROOM - NIGHT

Paramedics hover around Hart. Mia is on the floor
SOBBING, now handcuffed. One of the paramedics
announces -

                    PARAMEDIC #1
        We have a pulse!

                    POLICEMAN #1
        Clear the way people! Move it!

Hart is lifted onto a stretcher and carried from
the room.

                    SAVAGE
        What are the odds he lives?

                    PARAMEDIC #2
        Not good. Better start praying.

Savage stops as if slapped.

                    SAVAGE
        Don't count on it.

                    POLICEMAN #1
              (at Savage)
        Wait. Who the hell are you?

                    SAVAGE
        Savage. Journalist. I work for CNN.

                    POLICEMAN #2
            How'd you get here so fast?

                      FIELD
            Hey, you said your name was Melior!

                     HILLER
            You piece of shit. You liar!

Field pushes Savage. Hiller throws a punch. The
police intervene. They clear everyone from the house.

EXT. DRIVEWAY - NIGHT

The ambulance pulls away. Mia is placed into a
squad car.

EXT. DRIVEWAY - SAME

                     SAVAGE
            Our money is inside that house.

                    POLICEMAN #1
            What money?

                     HILLER
            Millions.

                    POLICEMAN #2
            What's going on here? Gambling?

                     SAVAGE
            No, it's an exclusive retreat.

                    POLICEMAN #2
            A retreat?

                     SAVAGE
            Workshop. For enlightenment.

                    POLICEMAN #1
                  (at his partner)
            My bet says illegal gambling.

                    HILLER
Absolutely not, Officer.

                    TOBIN
Gentleman, I can explain.

                    POLICEMAN #1
Who are you?

                    TOBIN
Tobin. Melvin. The billionaire? I'm
the founder and CEO of InnerChip.

                    POLICEMAN #1
Harry, call for backup. Now!

                    TOBIN
Wait, that's not necessary.

The policemen unclasp their guns and gets them to
back up.

                    POLICEMAN #1
I don't know what kind of operation
you're running here, but I suspect
it's something unlawful. Tell your
story at the police station.

                    ZIT
We get a phone call, yeah?

                    POLICEMAN #1
One call.

The band members SLAP high-fives. In unison they say -

                    PISS
Brady!

                    POLICEMAN #2
Who's Brady?

FIELD
This is bad. Not good. No...

Suzzie grabs and hugs Michele

                    SUZZIE
          I don't want to go to jail.

                    MICHELE
          We won't.

                    POLICEMAN #1
          You will if you don't start talking.

Natalie hands the officer a brochure from her
purse.

                    NATALIE
          Extreme Nirvana. The reason we are
          all here. Stupid, right?

                    POLICEMAN #1
          You're joking.

Natalie redirects his eyes from her breasts to
the brochure.

                    NATALIE
          You are able to read, yes?

He GRUMBLES but, enamored by her smile, starts
to read.

                    POLICEMAN #1
          I'll be god-damned. Harry, come look
          at this. Whole world's gone nuts.

The police huddle by their car, flipping through
the pages.

                    POLICEMAN #1
               (into radio)
          Cancel backup. Roger that. Over.

His partner claps his hands and raises his voice saying -

> POLICEMAN #2
> Listen up, statements from everyone!

EXT. DRIVEWAY - NIGHT

Limousines are packed with luggage. The attendees are being driven away. Field, Savage, and Hiller confront Deke.

> HILLER
> Our money. We want it.

> DEKE
> Nobody gets nothing tonight. The police confiscated it as evidence.

Savage shakes out another cigarette.

> DEKE
> Look on the bright side. If Hart lives, you can sue him in court.

> FIELD
> A lawsuit? No way. I-I can't.

Field, mentally imploding, veers off to sit on his luggage.

> SAVAGE
> I just might sue your ass too.

> DEKE
> (sneers)
> Good luck with that.

Hiller adjusts his glasses and walks over to Dorothy.

> HILLER
> This kind of publicity could make me a laughing stock.

Dorothy kisses him on the cheek.

> DOROTHY
> I know, Dear. Stay calm.

> HILLER
> (whispers)
> At first I thought she had used my
> gun. Thank God it wasn't mine.

EXT. INTERNATIONAL AIRPORT - NIGHT

Planes taxi along the runway - planes landing,
taking off.

> HART (V.O.)
> So my flock left me. With their
> bewildered psychic tails tucked
> between their enlightened legs.
> With one exception.

INT. BACK SEAT, TOBIN'S LIMOUSINE - NIGHT

Natalie is beside Tobin. He places the engagement
ring on her finger. Kissing him, she moves a hand
between his legs.

> NATALIE
> I was overwhelmed by it all.

> TOBIN
> I never understood why you wanted us
> to come in the first place.

> NATALIE
> To make certain I loved you. I do.

> TOBIN
> I can only hope you mean that.

> NATALIE
> You're my knight in shining armor,
> Melvy. My stallion. My stud.

                    TOBIN
                (whispers)
        And you, you're my Lady Godiva.

                    NATALIE
                (pouts)
        It's not fair you get to pluck my
        precious jewel for free, when I'm
        forced to sign a silly prenuptial.

                    TOBIN
        Natalie, my attorney insisted -

                    NATALIE
        What about your wife?

                    TOBIN
        If you love me it shouldn't matter.

                    NATALIE
        That would be my line.

                    TOBIN
        My attorney was pretty firm.

Tobin squirms pleasurably at the stroke of
Natalie's hand.

                    NATALIE
        When I ride you bareback, you get
        very firm. Be firm for me, Melvy.

                    TOBIN
        Natalie... Okay, all right... I -

INT. BAR, AIRPORT - NIGHT

Seated in a lounge, holding drinks, are Suzzie
and Michele.

                    SUZZIE
        No longer will we be ugly on the
        inside. We'll be pretty inside out.

                    141

                    MICHELE
You're talking nonsense again.

                    SUZZIE
I want us to be more charitable.

A passing businessman stops to boldly sit at
their table.

                     MAN
You two ladies are truly gorgeous. Do
you mind if I join you?

                   TOGETHER
     Yes.

His smile turns ugly. He stands and snarls -

                     MAN
I lied. You're both witches!

INT. AIRPLANE, SKY - NIGHT

A woman is seated next to Russ Field and asks -

                    WOMAN
You're awfully quiet.

He looks at her suspiciously.

                    FIELD
Are you... You're not one of them,
are you? Some kind of plant?

                    WOMAN
         (humored)
A plant? No, I'm a woman.

                    FIELD
No, I meant... A spy.

                    WOMAN
Espionage? Is that your field.

                    FIELD
Field, no. He ruins people's lives.
Excuse me. I'm not really myself, not
anymore. Someone died and I -

                    WOMAN
I'm sorry.

                    FIELD
          (shrugs it off)

The woman takes hold of the book in her lap. She
focuses on the multitude of scratches on his face.

                    WOMAN
What happened to your face?

                    FIELD
I know. I can't even recognize myself
either. I've been changed.

                    WOMAN
Did you want to talk about it?

                    FIELD
          (effusive)
I underwent a spiritual enema. I
know, it sounds crazy. This retreat
to cleanse your karma. I've done bad
things. Out of greed. But I'm going
to change. Surrender myself.

                    WOMAN
Good. Okay, I'm going to read now.

INT. AIRPORT TERMINAL - NIGHT

Brady, the manager for PISS, is pissed, pacing.
He sees PISS exit the airline gate.

                    BRADY
Not once did you call me!

                    BRADY (cont.)
        Bloody hell. What happened? Don't
        answer. No! Stop smiling!

EXT. HOUSE, ENTRANCE - EVENING

Holding flowers, Will Savage opens the door and
enters.

INT. HOUSE, LIVING ROOM - NIGHT

Two woman are snuggled together on a sofa watching a movie.
                    SAVAGE (O.C.)
        Emily.

                    EMILY
        Will. What are you doing here?

                    SAVAGE
        Leslie.

                    LESLIE
        Hello, Will.

                    SAVAGE
        Emily, I've loved you from the day we
        met. And I've said things that were
        wrong. And behaved badly. I can do
        better. Please let me try.
            (at the TV screen)
        Unforgiven? I love this movie.

                    EMILY
        Will, this is not about Viagra. It's
        about feelings. You're crying.

Savage starts to deny it but lets the tears fall
freely.

                    EMILY
        I've never seen you this emotional.

LESLIE
And so vulnerable.

SAVAGE
You made me. Feel. Like a eunuch.

Both women sigh. They get up and smother him with hugs.

INT. BEDROOM, THE HILLER RESIDENCE - NIGHT

Dorothy and Harold Hiller are kissing and embracing in bed.

DOROTHY
I feel like a virgin.
(giggles)
It's been so long. I wonder if we've forgotten how to do this.

EXT. DRIVEWAY, Z-BLISS ESTATE - SAME NIGHT

Deke, Jake, Jess, and the same policemen and paramedics who were there earlier, are back. Beside their cars, they are drinking beers and celebrating, and LAUGHING.

INT. BOARD ROOM, INNERCHIP CORPORATION - DAY

Employees are gathered around a table. They stare with open mouths at Melvin Tobin standing in a white robe.

TOBIN
This will be our new dress code.
Am I sensing negative energy?

INT. DARKENED ROOM, LOCATION UNKNOWN - DAY / NIGHT

CLOSEUP ON HART'S FACE, motionless as a corpse, with the hint of a smile. In a state of eternal bliss, at peace.

145

                    HART (V.O.)
So, what became of me? I survived.
Miraculously. I'm lying. Everything
went according to plan. Almost. And
I'm a changed man. To a degree.

PULL BACK as Hart's eyes open. His smile broadens.

The naked backside of an unidentified WOMAN
comes into view along with pleasurable MOANS.
She straddled on top of Hart.

                    HART
You can put that thing away now.
You've made your point. I was bad.

A riding crop is TOSSED to the floor.

                    HART
Our life together will be bliss.

The tone of her MURMUR is suspicious.

                    HART
We really do have chemistry.

The MURMUR becomes a soft LAUGH.

                    HART
I know, coming from me, a fraud? That
said, I'd never lie to you.

CLOSE on MIA with an smitten grin.

                    MIA
Shut up. I want to enjoy this.

THREE MONTHS LATER

INT. POOL, Z-BLISS ESTATE - DAY

Mia sips a margarita and looks at Hart, relaxing
in a chair. He give her a smile. A wedding ring
shines on her finger.

> MIA
> It's hard to believe. No process
> servers pounding the gates.

> HART
> You worry too much.

> MIA
> As an equal partner, shouldn't I?

> HART
> I keep going back to that night you
> shot me. You even had me convinced.
> (sips his drink)
> You're an incredibly good actress.

> MIA
> I'm not.

> HART
> Take the compliment.

> MIA
> I can't.

> HART
> Don't be difficult.

> MIA
> I wanted to kill you.

> HART
> (processing this)

> MIA
> Anyway, your plan worked.

Mia sorts through several news items from a file
in her lap.

                    MIA
Can you believe all this? Look.

MAGAZINE: "PISS ON LOVE. STRANGE NEW ALBUM. RAVE
REVIEWS"

                    MIA
And this one, from these two.

HEADLINE: "SOCIALITES WIN HEARTS BY SAVING SOCIAL
SERVICES"

                    MIA
And Field. He publically credits you
for his epiphany. He confessed - even
apologized - to those he defrauded.
He's later quoted as saying: "I've
never felt so free."
         (beat)
He said this from prison.

                    HART
Multiple realities. Strange world.

                    MIA
And this guy, I thought for sure he'd
come after us. But he sends a blank
letter with these. Explain.

INSERT - THREE PLAYING CARDS, ALL THEM ARE THE
QUEEN OF HEARTS

                    HART
Three Queens. That would make a good
hand. Often a winning one.

                    MIA
He got fired at CNN.

                    HART
I'm guessing this matters more.

MIA
What are you not telling me?

HART
That maybe all this was a miracle.

Hart displays a bemused smile. Mia holds up a POSTCARD.

MIA
And who's this from? No message. I'm guessing from her, your lover?

PHOTO OF A LIFESAVER FLOTATION DEVISE ALONE IN THE OCEAN.

HART
(laughs)
She did prove to be our wild card.

Hart sips his drink and shrugs.

HART
I have a confession. I may have averted the backlash by donating the retreat money to charities.

MIA
All of the money?

HART
Would you like to whip me again?

MIA
You didn't. Did you?

HART
(toasts her)
I kept a substantial retainer fee.

MIA
I've created a monster.

> HART
> Let's not aim so high next time. That
> one got a bit out of control.

> MIA
> You think?

> HART
> I didn't consult you. You're angry.

> MIA
> No. I only wanted you to love me.

A phone on a table RINGS. Mia takes a breath,
picks it up.

> MIA
> (cheerfully)
> Z-Bliss. How can we help you?

She maintains a cheerfully optimistic disposition.

> MIA
> He survived. That's right. He's recu-
> perating. Undergoing therapy. Yes,
> he's a very fortunate man.

Mia makes a face and sticks out her tongue at Hart.

> MIA
> We have. Reconciled. Happily, yes.
> He's nearly recovered. Thank you.

Hart toasts the mystery caller with his margarita.

INT. OFFICE, HILLER & ASSOCIATES - DAY

Hiller is behind his large desk, fidgeting with a
gold pen.

On the desk top are newspaper articles with highlighted text.

                    HILLER
    I'll cut to the chase. I normally
    don't do this sort of thing, but...
            (removes glasses)
    I have a client. An important one. I
    mentioned your retreat. How it helped
    me and Dorothy. Listen...

INT. POOL, Z-BLISS ESTATE - DAY

Mia's mouth opens wide, aghast. Hart mouths -

                    HART
    What?

INT. OFFICE, HILLER & ASSOCIATES - DAY

Hiller picks up another newspaper article.

                    HILLER
    That donation you made. First rate.
    Demonstrated to me enormous class.

Hiller starts doodling with his pen.

                    HILLER
    The point is, this is very hush-hush.
    Top secret. It's for a person who
    holds the highest office.

CLOSEUP on Hiller doodling STARS and STRIPES.

                    HILLER
    The President. Yes. He wants to
    arrange one of those exclusive
    retreats. The extreme kind. We all
    feel he's in need of enlightenment.
    Naturally, I thought to call you.
            (long pause)
    Hello?

                                    THE END

                        151